MEET ME
AT THE
BOATHOUSE

Also by Suzanne Bugler

Staring Up at the Sun

MEET ME
AT THE
BOATHOUSE

Suzanne Bugler

*Hodder
Children's
Books*

A division of Hachette Children's Books

A Catalogue record for this book is available from the British Library

ISBN-13: 978 0 340 93229 2

Typeset in Goudy Old Style by Avon DataSet Ltd,
Bidford-on-Avon, Warwickshire

Printed in the UK by CPI Bookmarque, Croydon, CR0 4TD

The paper and board used in this paperback by Hodder Children's Books
are natural recyclable products made from wood grown in
sustainable forests. The manufacturing processes conform to the
environmental regulations of the country of origin.

Hodder Children's Books
A division of Hachette Children's Books
338 Euston Road
London NW1 3BH

For Matthew and Alex

1

Danny told me there were seven manor houses in Eppingham. I didn't really believe him but I went along with it anyway, just for a laugh.

Everything was a laugh with Danny, when he was in a good mood.

He said we were going on a magical mystery tour and that he was going to show me Eppingham as I had never seen it before, starting with the seven manor houses. We set off from his house and walked up the back way, cutting across the footbridge over the watersplash and following the main road up past the blackberry fields and the reservoir till we were right up the far end of Eppingham. Then we worked our way back down, snaking through the streets, stopping at this weird house and that weird house. Manor houses one to six. You could see they weren't really manor houses – one of them was just an old two-up-two-down slapped in the middle of a terrace of other old two-up-two-downs – but Danny had spotted some little quirk on each of these houses that marked them out somehow. And he'd got a story about every one. He said the biggish house on the corner of London Road used to be owned by a nutter who kept a pet lion, locked up in one of the bedrooms. Then one day the lion escaped and ate the man, then got out the house and bit the milkman. Up and down the High Street it ran, causing havoc, till the army came in, and shot it.

'Don't you remember that?' he said. 'It was in all the papers.'

I didn't remember, but I half killed myself laughing.

'And that one there,' he said, when we came to manor house number three, halfway down Water Lane, 'is the creepiest house in Eppingham. No one stays there for long.' It was an old, mock-Tudor house separated from the newish semis on both sides of it by a crowd of overgrown bushes. The window frames were painted black and there was a For Sale sign stuck out the front. 'The man that lived there, years ago, found out his wife was cheating on him. One night, when she was sleeping, he got an axe out of the shed, and hacked her up. Cut her head right off.' Sunlight sparked off the blue of Danny's eyes as he spoke, and he lashed at the air with his hands for emphasis. Sometimes you'd think he really believed his own stories. 'And then he hung himself. From that tree there.' He pointed to the oak tree that dominated the front garden, darkening the house.

Of course I didn't believe him. But even so,

I felt goosepimples break out across my skin.

He even had a story about the two-up-two-down. 'Gold taps,' he said. 'And gold handles on all the doors. Solid gold. Even the loo is gold,' he said, 'and all the pipes. The old woman that lives there is loaded.'

The seventh manor house was just along the river from the watersplash at the end of Danny's road. We'd worked our way back to where we started when he said, 'Here. Down here.' He took my hand and pulled me along behind him, slowly. We climbed off the bridge and down into the reeds where the river started to bend round; the reeds looked like they grew straight out of the water and I thought we'd sink at any moment. He held my hand tight and we trod carefully. The river bank curved round and thickened out; soon we were clambering on harder ground, battling our way through nettles and brambles and weeds till we came against a fence of tangled wire. And suddenly there it was, the seventh house. A huge grey building that no one could possibly live in, with great dark windows that had cracks across the panes, and splits in the timbers where the roof had buckled. I'd never even known the house was there; you'd never see it from the road with all those trees packed up around it.

I thought that would be it. I thought we'd just see it and go, but Danny kept hold of my hand, and kept pulling me on.

'Keep down,' he said. 'There's an old guy lives there.' Crouching low, we skirted the edge of the fence, peeling our way through the overgrown grass that flicked in our faces, till we came to a gap where the wire had been pushed out, making a hole. 'I'm going to take you to a secret place,' he said, whispering as if he thought someone might hear. 'Somewhere no one else knows about. My secret place.'

His breath tickled my ear as he spoke and again the goosebumps rose up on the back of my neck.

'Come on,' he said and we squeezed our way through the hole in the fence, and then we were running like mad across the grounds because the old man that lived in the house had a dog, and the dog saw us or heard us or sniffed us out or whatever and started barking from in the depths of that house like a dog from hell . . . Danny had hold of my hand so tight that if I'd slowed for a second I'd have lost my fingers; my chest was burning and I didn't breathe at all till we were on the other side, past the house.

And then we were scrambling through more brambles, trying to dodge the thorns and nettles that grew high as our elbows. The remains of a wooden fence had been stacked up against the wire one behind it, the planks interwoven and held in place by straggling ivy. A little way along there was a broken, half boarded-over gateway. Still holding on to each other we clambered up and over, and came down on the other side, down into the cool damp weeds, and we lay there for a moment catching our breath and listening to the hammering of our hearts and to that dog, barking away.

Suddenly Danny started laughing. His face was flushed from running and from the heat of the sun, making his eyes seem even more blue. I laughed too, out of relief more than anything else, that we'd got past that dog alive. I didn't like to think about the journey back.

He rolled onto his front, propping himself up on one elbow and looking down at me. My heart, having slowed, started to speed up again now, as it always did when he looked at me like that. He smiled at me a sly, lazy smile. 'Almost there,' he said, and kissed me once, quickly, on the mouth. Then he was up on his feet again, and I followed him, back down to the edge of the river and along the bank, through the sweeping curtains of willow branches. We were far away from the road. Far away from everything. Once that dog stopped barking there was no sound except the humming of the bees and the swishing of the willows as we pushed our way through.

Then Danny stopped.

'Here it is,' he said. 'My secret place.'

We'd come to a dilapidated old boathouse, propped against the bank of a tiny inlet almost completely hidden by the trees. Part of the roof was missing where the wood had rotted through and the whole thing looked as if it might collapse into the river at any moment. There'd been three steps up to the entrance from the bank, but only one of them remained. I followed Danny in, careful to tread only on the edge of that step, in case it gave way. Inside, water lapped under the broken slats of the floor, and sunlight streamed through the gaps in the roof, lighting up the dust specs that danced in the air. Cobwebs hung from the roof, catching in my hair, and the air stank of mildew and rats. Yet in the sunshine it seemed so beautiful somehow, and so utterly, utterly peaceful.

'No one knows about this place except me,' Danny said. 'And now you.'

He showed me where he'd carved his name into the floor, in the wood just inside the entrance. Now he took his penknife out his pocket and underneath his own name he scratched *and Louise, forever*, into the wood. And then he drew a box around our names, digging his knife into the wood; sharp lines, closing us in.

Suddenly, he'd gone all serious.

'You and me, Louise,' he said, and the sunlight glinted off the blade of the knife and his eyes, simultaneously. 'Forever. That's how it's going to be. You and me.'

2

I used to walk past the end of Danny's road on my way to school. That's how it started. One morning I walked past and there he was waiting for me.

'All right if I walk with you?' he asked, and I suppose I felt flattered. He was dead good-looking in a wild sort of way, and he had the most gorgeous smile. I'd seen him around before; he was in Year Eleven the same as me but I'd never spoken to him or anything. I'd never had anything to do with him at school, because I was in the top stream for everything, and Danny wasn't. In fact Danny quite often didn't even go to school at all.

Still, he seemed to know a lot about me.

Later, when I'd known him for a while, he told me that was because he'd done his homework. He'd had it all planned, he said. He'd known for ages that I would be his; it was just a matter of timing.

He knew I was into athletics and loved running. He had maths when I had PE, he said, and sometimes he'd watch me, sprinting round the field. He knew who my friends were, though he wasn't sure about their names.

'That blonde one,' he said. 'Always tossing her hair over her shoulder like she thinks she's a horse. Carrie something.'

'Cara,' I said, laughing.

'You want to watch her,' he said. 'She's dead jealous of you.'

'Don't be daft,' I said. I'd known Cara for years. What would she be jealous of me for? And anyway, what did Danny know about it?

He looked at me, and I had the weird feeling that he knew rather a lot.

'And the other one, the dark-haired one with the glasses, who'd like you to disappear so she can have Cara all to herself? What's her name?'

'Emma,' I said, smiling at his perception. Not that I really believed him or anything, but still.

Then we talked about music, finding all these bands we had in common. He seemed to like everything I liked. He had this really cute way of using his hands a lot as he talked, fingers splayed, turning them in the air. He had long fingers, very white and flat knuckled. And I liked the way he spoke. He looked like he would have a bit of a rough voice but he didn't. He had a lovely voice, like an actor.

He walked with me to the junction at the top of the High Street, then he said, 'Uh-oh, here comes Cara.'

Sure enough, there she was in the distance, coming up her road. We met here most mornings, except when her dad gave her a lift. She kept flicking her hair back as she walked. Danny was right, she did look a bit like a horse.

'Well I'll be off then,' Danny said, and suddenly I wished that Cara had got herself a lift.

'You don't have to go,' I said. 'You can walk with us.'

'I think not,' Danny said, and gave me a wry smile. He had a gorgeous smile, and the most incredible eyes. 'Somehow I don't think Cara would approve of me,' he said, and then he was gone, off down the High Street. I wondered if he intended going to school. He'd certainly make himself late, going that way.

After that he was there every school day morning, bar a few, waiting for me. And soon he started waiting for me at the gates, too, at the end of the day, and walking home with me. If I came out of school with Cara – which was most days, except Wednesdays when she had Orchestra and Thursdays when I did athletics – he'd keep back, and follow us to the top of the High Street, where Cara and I split to go our separate ways. He'd stay behind till Cara was right out of sight, and then he'd catch me up.

Cara had no idea.

It seemed important to Danny, somehow, that it was secret.

On our way home one day, after about a week or so of walking together, we stopped at the point where we normally parted and Danny said, 'Do you want to come back for a cup of tea?'

It took me seconds to work out how much time I'd got, that there was half an hour maximum between the time I ought to get home and the time that I'd start being missed.

'OK,' I said, knowing I'd be late back, knowing I'd have to run, and then lie. He lived right down the end of Acacia Avenue, near the watersplash. It's not a road I'd ever been down much, not since I was a little kid and my dad used to take me down to the watersplash with my fishing net, to catch newts. As we walked our fingers touched, and Danny caught at my hand, and held it. I felt a charge from his fingertips, like electricity. He felt it too, I know he did; he squeezed my hand, tight.

There was no one in at his house. He took a key out from under the pot by the back door and let us into the kitchen. When he pushed open the back door a cat jumped down from the table and slithered past us, out the door. Breakfast things were piled up beside the sink and someone had been to Sainsbury's, and left the bags stacked on the floor, waiting to be unpacked.

No one was in, but even so when we'd made the tea we took it upstairs to his bedroom.

'Welcome to my humble abode,' he said, closing the door behind us. His room was tiny, and cramped with just his bed and a small chest of drawers, and his CDs piled up on the floor next to his CD player. There was an ashtray on the floor beside his bed, heaped up with cigarette butts, and stuffed in the corner behind the door was a pile of clothes; socks and things. I could smell the ashtray, and the socks.

I sat on his bed next to him, and sipped at my tea, too quickly, burning my mouth. I could feel him watching me, even as he leaned forward to put his own cup on top of the drawers. He was watching, and waiting. My heart started to beat hard and fast; I couldn't meet his eye and again I sipped at that too-hot tea. I wished he'd say something; it was the silence that was making me nervous, that and the way he was staring at me. Then he took the cup out of my hand, peeling my fingers away from the china with his own, one by one. He put my cup down on the floor, and I remember thinking I'd have to be careful not to kick it over. He turned back to face me and now I did look at him, at his face as he moved towards me. Our eyes locked and held, till we were too close, too close to see anything and then his mouth was on mine, paper-dry and soft, barely touching. He put his hands on my arms, holding me still, though I couldn't have moved if I'd wanted to. I could barely even breathe. He kissed me carefully, like he was holding back, kiss after kiss, pressing his mouth against mine yet holding his body away from me till I could hardly stand it.

Then suddenly he stopped.

I'd have gone on kissing him forever. But he pulled away from me, and he laughed, nervously, as if it had been a mistake or something. He let go of my arms and started groping under his bed for his cigarettes and his lighter; he offered me one but all I could do was shake my head. He leaned forward with his elbows resting on his knees, and tapped his cigarette three times against the back of his hand before sticking it in his mouth, and lighting it. Then he drew in deeply, and held his breath for a moment before letting the smoke out in short, controlled bursts. He had an old-fashioned metal lighter with a flip-top lid that he clicked open and shut, open and shut with the fingers of one hand, before letting the lighter drop idly to the floor between his feet.

'What's the matter?' I asked, desperate to break the silence.

He took another long drag on his cigarette and slowly

let the smoke back out on a sigh. 'It's us,' he said at last. 'You and me.' He stared at his cigarette, flicking it from side to side between his fingers in a no-no-no gesture. 'It wouldn't work.'

'Why not?' Panic sharpened my voice. How could he make me want him like that, and then just pull away?

'You know why not, Louise,' he said, but I didn't. I didn't have a clue.

I had to just go in the end.

I had to just leave him there in his bedroom, staring at the floor, and let myself out. There was a hollow inside me, a huge punch hole. I ran home, all the way, fast. I ran because I was late, and because the air against me would rush off the smell of Danny's cigarette smoke, and dry the tears right out of my eyes.

My mum was in the kitchen with Mrs Crosby from next door when I got back. They were sitting at the table, heads bent over the tea pot, deep in gossip. I could see them through the glass of the door. I wiped my face clean of all feeling, and walked in.

They looked up from the table in unison; like they were puppets, with their head strings tied to the door.

'Ah, here she is now,' said my mum, so straight away I knew they'd been talking about me, though there is nothing new in that.

'You're late, Louise,' Mrs Crosby said, with the gleam

of anticipation in her eye. 'Your mum was getting worried about you.'

'I was talking to Cara,' I lied in my blankest, blandest voice.

Mrs Crosby looked from me to my mother, practically squirming in her chair over the prospect of a little domestic drama. But whatever it was they'd been saying about me proved more interesting to my mother than the real and disappointing me in person, because she just said, 'Well hurry up then, Louise. Haven't you got homework to do?'

Danny wasn't there the next morning, or the next.

I looked out for him at school but I didn't see him, and on Saturday I went for a walk, right down his road and past his house, to the watersplash, hoping I might bump into him.

I didn't.

Then on Sunday night just as I was going to bed, I went to draw my curtains and looked out of my window and there he was. Sitting on the garden wall of the house across the road, smoking a cigarette. He'd have seen my light go on but he didn't look up. For ages he sat there, long after he'd crushed the butt of that cigarette out with his foot. I turned my light off again, but he still didn't look up. He just sat there, for ages and ages while I stared down at him. I heard my mum and dad going up to bed, and the creaking of the house settling down, while still he just sat there. Then, still without looking up at me, he stood up, and walked away.

I walked to school on my own again on Monday morning. I knew I wouldn't see Danny. There was a small, tight lump down in my chest. It seemed to me that it was over before it had even started, but no matter, I'd get over it.

There were plenty of other boys.

Cara and Emma and I were chatting to some of those other boys at lunchtime when I caught sight of Danny right across the far side of the playground, watching me. Automatically I smiled at him but he didn't smile back. So I turned my smile on Jacob instead, and laughed at the story he was telling us, like it was just the funniest thing.

'And then the whole lot fell down, missing Mrs Rivers by a fraction,' Jacob was saying, and I clapped my hand over my mouth.

'Yeah, it was well funny,' Miles said. 'You had to be there.'

Cara laughed too, and gave them the full benefit of her hair, letting it fall forward over her face and then flicking it right back again. Several strands attached themselves to Miles's shoulder. Deliberate, of course.

I glanced across the playground again at Danny. He was still standing there, watching. *See me having fun*, I thought. *See if I don't need you.*

After all, two can play games.

And the game worked, I suppose, because Danny was waiting at the gates when Cara and I came out of school. I ignored him of course, and walked with Cara to the end of her road. I knew he was behind us, following. I could sense him. More than sense him. I could feel him there, like a magnetic force.

I walked dead slowly after Cara and I split, so that he could catch me up. And when he did, I speeded up a little. I didn't even look at him, at first.

'Hi, how are you?' he asked, with real concern in his voice, which I took to mean that he expected me to be distraught after his weird rejection on Thursday. Well obviously I wasn't going to let him carry on thinking that.

'I'm fine thanks,' I replied brightly, and as off-hand as I could manage, like I'd almost forgotten who he was.

'Good, good,' he said, and that was it, till we were right up near to his road. The silence was agony, but I didn't think it was up to me to break it. Even so, I found myself slowing down when we got to the top of his road. I didn't want to leave things like that. So strung out in thin air.

'What's going on with you and Jacob Warren?' he asked suddenly, stopping. He placed one hand on my arm, pinning me in.

'Nothing,' I said. I was looking at his face but I couldn't quite see his eyes. The sun was right behind him, blinding me.

'It didn't look like nothing to me.'

I squinted up into his face, straining to see his eyes but they were blackened out by the sunlight, hidden. 'Well it was nothing,' I said. 'He's just a mate.'

He dropped his hand away from my arm. I felt the loss of it more than I'd felt it being there, which is wrong, I know. I wanted it fencing me in, claiming me.

Suddenly he lifted his hand and traced his fingers over my face. Still I couldn't see his eyes, though I could feel them, staring right inside of me. 'You're too good for me, Louise,' he said, in the saddest voice. Then he kissed me gently on the cheek, and turned and walked away.

It hollowed me out inside.

How can you not be good enough for someone because you're too good for them? How ridiculous is that? I walked on like I didn't care, and I didn't look back, even though I knew he'd expect me to. And I tried to tell myself he was right, I was too good for him.

But it didn't work. I mean, that really was too stupid for words. I could feel the tears building, hot in my chest.

How could I be too good for anyone?

I tried to put him out of my head.

I'd be mad to get involved with Daniel Fisher anyway. He was a loser; he was a dope-head, for God's sake. I'd never have even come this far if he hadn't started it. I'd have steered well clear.

I lay on my bed that night and tried to forget him. I tried to forget the way he'd kissed me, and the way he'd held me – like he didn't want to get too close, and break me.

I tried to forget the way he made me feel.

3

'Where's your boyfriend?' Cara asked, somewhat snootily, when I met her at the traffic lights the next morning.

I was so late I was surprised she'd even waited for me, and I wasn't in the mood for sarcasm. Silence, I thought, would be my safest bet, so I walked on fast beside her, saying nothing.

But Cara wasn't giving up. 'Daniel Fisher,' she went on, saying his name like it tasted bad in her mouth. 'Where is he this morning then?'

'I don't know,' I muttered. 'And he isn't my boyfriend.'

Cara snorted. 'I've seen you walking with him. And I've seen him trotting off as soon as I appear, like it's some big secret.' Cara could be catty, sometimes, if she felt snubbed. But I did feel a bit guilty; after all, you shouldn't keep secrets from your best friend.

I was going to try and explain but then she got in there before me. 'What's the matter, did you think I'd try and steal him from you? Is that it?' Again she snorted. 'Well believe me, you've got no worries there.'

And she flounced off ahead, walking even faster, so I had to practically jog to keep up with her.

So then I had Cara in a nark to deal with too. The best thing to do about that was just be ultra nice and pander to her, which I did, in spade-loads.

'It's really nothing,' I said to her later, when we came out of English at lunchtime. 'He just walked with me a few times, that's all.' She looked at me sideways, unconvinced. 'I walk past his road,' I justified, and that seemed to do it a little. After all, she hadn't known that. She wouldn't have known where Daniel Fisher lived.

'Look,' I said, stopping at the bottom of the stairs on our way out. 'If it was anything more than that I'd have told you. Wouldn't I?'

Cara stopped too, and looked me in the eyes for a few seconds, making up her mind. I held her stare, doing my best to keep my own eyes totally blank. Then she sighed and dropped her head to one side and gave me a faint, wounded smile. And she got in one last jibe, just in case.

'Yeah, well,' she said. 'I didn't think your taste was quite that bad.'

But I still had to be punished.

All day Cara favoured Emma with her chat and her charm, and remained just that little bit too chilly towards me. Emma, of course, lapped it up. That's the trouble when there's three in a friendship. Danny was right about that, at least. Emma was nice and everything but she was always there, ready to step in and take my place. Which was sad really, because Cara and I had been best friends since we'd started at Eppingham High, and Emma didn't stand a chance against that. Sometimes Cara and I laughed about it, but sometimes it was annoying, particularly when Cara used it to her advantage.

Like now.

We were sitting on a bench near the football pitch, talking about the concert planned at the end of term. At least, they were talking. Some girl who used to go to our school was in a band, and they'd got a record out that had got into the charts. Not very high up or anything, but even so. And they were coming to play at our school; everyone was talking about it. Except not me, right then. I was sitting on the wrong side of Emma, talking to no one.

'We'll have to get there really early,' Emma was saying, all pally-pally to Cara. 'To get up near the front. It'll be packed out.'

'Do you think there'll be other people there? From outside school?'

'I don't know. Probably.'

Idly, I listened to them. I found myself wondering

where Danny was today, as he didn't appear to be in school. Then I stamped the thought out. What was the point in even caring?

'What you going to wear?' one of them said, I don't know who, and off they launched into a verbal trawl of their wardrobes.

'You'll have to come round to my house beforehand, to get ready and that,' Cara said and Emma fairly choked at the honour. 'Then we can go together.' Cara paused now, then made a big show of turning round slightly towards me. 'Oh you, too, Louise,' she said, pointedly late, like she'd just remembered I was there.

I had another friend before Cara. My real best friend, if you like. Natalie Banks. She was my best friend right through infants and juniors and she lived round the corner from us, in Fairview Drive, in a house with a big garden out the front, filled with the various undone pieces of her brother's cars. Natalie was allowed out on her own and she'd come round my house and we'd play outside with my mother watching from the house and saying *Isn't it time Natalie went home?* every five seconds. My mum never liked her though she was obsessed with her well enough, quizzing me all the time on what was Natalie's mother like? Was she at work? What was their house like? Was it tidy? What did they have for tea?

As if I cared.

When we left the juniors Natalie went to the Catholic school in Sandwell but I still saw her, after school and at weekends. We still talked about the same things. Not boys and clothes and hair, but other things, the dreams inside our heads.

But then Natalie was killed, along with her mother, in a car crash. Her brother told me, when I went round there. I thought he was making it up because he was a sad, sad sicko but still I went home shaking.

It turned out to be true. I heard my mum telling Mrs Crosby that Natalie's dad had gone half mad with grief, letting the house run to ruin, and had she seen the state of those curtains? But he packed up soon, and moved away. I saw their house, empty, windows like black eyes, and the For Sale sign out the front, Anchor and Co. Someone had written a W in front of the A.

Most of the time I managed to act like I'd forgotten about Natalie but sometimes I just couldn't. Sometimes when Cara could get such a strop on about something I had or hadn't done I really missed Natalie. With Natalie things just weren't such a big deal.

All in all I had a pretty miserable day. And when I got home the first thing my mum said to me was, 'I hear you've been out walking with a boy.'

I dropped my bag down by the door, got myself a glass down from the cupboard, and filled it at the sink. What kind of an expression is that? Out walking? My mum is from the Dark Ages. I drank the water, keeping my eyes on what I was doing, though I could feel her watching me. This could go either way.

'Mrs Crosby tells me she's seen you. Walking with a young man.' My mum quotes Mrs Crosby like she's a source of unquestionable knowledge, with direct access to the truth. When really Mrs Crosby is a nosy old bat, to be avoided at all costs.

Now I know it drives my mum mad when I say nothing, and give nothing away. But really, what else could I do when up against her and Mrs Crosby and their endless speculations over my life? It was the only way to keep them out.

'Well who is he, then, this young man? And where did you meet him?'

Still I said nothing. I mean, what did she expect? A whole background summary?

'Well at least bring him home and let us meet him,' my mum said, all hurt now, like I'd deliberately gone out and got myself a boyfriend, just so that I could keep him secret from her.

Bring Danny Fisher home? As if.

The trouble with my mum is that she has nothing to

do, except look after the house, and my dad, and me. She should get herself a job. My dad suggested that to her once.

'Why don't you get yourself a nice little job? Just part time. Something to keep you busy?'

God what a strop she went into after that.

'Don't you think I'm busy enough looking after you two all day?' she screeched. 'Don't you think I have enough to do?'

She sulked for days. It drove me nuts the way we had to pussyfoot around her. I remember coming back in from school one day to find her in the kitchen doing the ironing, attacking my dad's shirts like she wished he was still inside them. She'd got her mouth clamped shut, lips twitching, and her nose was all red.

She wanted me to ask what was wrong but I didn't. Instead I said, 'Dad's right. Maybe you should get a job.'

She slammed down the iron, singeing a burn right through my dad's white shirt and into the board. She didn't seem to notice the smell, or the smoke.

'How could I ever get a job?' she wailed, unsticking that iron and banging it back down again. 'What would I do? I've spent too long looking after you and now I'm too old.'

She was right about that. She *was* too old. My gran once told me my mum had longed for a baby for years and years and had almost given up hope when I came along, her little miracle. Only trouble was that little miracle didn't turn out to be such a good thing after all. My mum ended up having such a hard time giving birth to me that she's still getting over it, fifteen years later.

'It's her hormones,' my dad always says, by way of an excuse when she goes off into one of her total rages, screaming her head off, throwing things around.

It looks more like a bloody tantrum to me. Do you think if I behaved the way she did and tried to blame it on my hormones I'd get away with it? I don't think so.

I don't understand my mum, but I don't understand my dad either. What is it that makes him put up with her awful moods, *and* excuse them? Is it guilt? Guilt for not giving her a baby for so long and then getting her pregnant with *me*?

How do you think that makes me feel? I didn't ask to be born and yet it's my fault that my mum's such a mess and my dad's so pathetic.

Once, we were driving back from my auntie's house in Andover and my mum was going on and on, the usual stuff; why didn't my dad talk more, why did he just sit there while everyone else made all the effort, why did she have to be so stupid as to go and marry him in the first place?

I sat in the back, trying not to hear. But then I

accidentally caught sight of my dad's face in the mirror. He had tears rolling down his cheeks in an unchecked stream, and dripping off his chin. The shock of it was like a punch, right into my stomach. I looked out the window, not wanting to see.

I hated him for being so weak.

But that night my mum got what she wanted, somewhat sooner than I expected. I was up in my room after supper, doing my homework when I heard the doorbell ring. I barely took any notice but then I heard Danny's voice, down in the hall, and every hair on my head stood on end, every nerve sparked up. I heard him laugh, just the right laugh and though I couldn't make out the words I could hear the tone of his voice pitched exactly right; soothing. I wanted to hear what he was saying. I wanted to get up from where I lay sprawled across my bed with my books and listen at the door but I couldn't move. I was stuck, rigid, with my heart thumping in my chest.

Then I heard steps on the stairs; two lots of steps. Still I couldn't move. My door opened; I turned my head slow and dumb.

'You have a visitor,' my mum said with the puffed up voice of the newly charmed, and there he was, right beside her, the charmer. He had a look on his face that would fool anyone and a stash of CDs in his arms.

'Half an hour, Louise,' my mum stipulated, her voice gurgled up with a heady load of I told you sos, which she trotted back downstairs to share with my dad, leaving Danny and me alone.

He closed the door behind him and the clock started ticking.

'I brought you some CDs,' he said, keeping up the act, for the benefit of anyone who might still be listening.

I didn't reply. I couldn't. I was too stunned that Daniel Fisher was right there in my bedroom.

He smiled a nervous smile, disarming me. 'Can I sit down?' he asked and I sat up, scrunching up my books underneath me. He sat on the bed beside me, so close I could smell him; the warm tobacco smell of his leather jacket and the tang of the gel in his hair. My heart kept up its hard, warning beat.

'Here,' he said, and he passed the CDs from his hands into mine. I held them, feeling where the plastic had got hot under his fingers. 'I want you to listen to them. There's something on them . . . on all of them . . . that reminds me of you. I put a cross by the tracks,' he said. He moved as if to show me, then stopped, mid-turn and changed his mind. Then he slumped forward, elbows on his knees, head hidden in his hands.

'It's no good,' he murmured, so quiet I could barely hear him, and the fear of loss ripped through me. 'I shouldn't have come.'

I put the CDs down on the floor and stared at the back of his head. His hair was a dark blonde colour, almost brown. Sometimes, in the right light, it looked gold. I ached to touch him. I reached out to touch his arm; my hand felt heavy, charged. He caught at my fingers with his own, and held them.

'It'll never work,' he said, turning to look at me with the saddest eyes. 'You and me . . .' he pulled at my fingers, twisting them with his own. And then he said it again. 'You're too good for me.'

'How can you say that?' It was the stupidest thing to say, the stupidest. I clawed my fingers against his, stilling them. 'It's just so not true.'

'It is true, Louise,' he said. In the dim light of my room his pupils were enormous; dark hypnotic pits. I wanted to be lost in the endless, endless black. 'You could do much better than me.' His voice was a blanket, weighing me down. 'You could have anyone you wanted.'

'I want you.' It came out like a promise. The words hung between us; given.

He untwined his fingers from mine and raised his hand to touch my hair, gently pushing it back from my cheek. Our eyes were locked; I could not look away. I didn't want to look away. I was gazing into the abyss; I was on a cliff edge, preparing to jump. His fingers wove into my hair, catching onto the tangles, till he had his hand cupping the back of my head. I could not move. I could only stare into the place inside his eyes as he brought his face closer, blocking out everything.

This time he didn't stop kissing me. This time the kissing went on and on, with his hand round my head, holding me. I couldn't breathe; I couldn't think. He tipped me back onto the bed so he was on top of me, and his hands were in between us, struggling with clothes. I could hear the TV droning away downstairs and my heart was thumping, thumping. He'd got his hands inside my tights, pushing them down; I felt a ladder pop and run. My tights got caught round my ankles and I used one foot to free the other, and I felt his belt clunk cold against my thigh as he hoiked it undone. My hands were on his back, inside his top. He was looking at me and I was looking at him and he'd got one leg between mine, nudging them apart. I could feel the prickle of his skin against mine, and his heart, hammering away, fast as my own. We were close, that close.

Then he was still suddenly, poised. He had that question in his eyes and there was this voice inside my head saying go on, go on, just do it. I let my legs fall open slightly. He had this look on his face like the sweetest, sweetest pain. Gently, gently he started nudging it in. Still I could hear the TV and my ears were ringing from the strain of listening for any movement from downstairs. In he pushed, and it did hurt a bit. I grabbed at his shoulders. He stopped a second then pushed again. Then all of a sudden he was pulling out of me, fast. I felt the heat, pumping onto my thigh, and then this disbelief, this what have I done?

He collapsed on top of me for a second and I felt so detached, like it had been some kind of dare. Wait till I tell Cara, I thought. But I knew I wouldn't tell her. I wouldn't tell anyone. I couldn't believe what I'd done.

We needed something to wipe it all off my thigh. Embarrassed now, at being half naked, I grabbed my nightshirt from under my pillow and used that.

'Well . . .' Danny said. 'I wasn't expecting that.'

A door opened downstairs. Lightning fast I scrambled to get dressed. Danny did the same.

'Louise,' my dad called from downstairs. 'Time for your friend to go now. You've got homework to do.'

Danny put his hand against the side of my face and kissed my mouth, soft, slow. There was a jackhammer in my heart that hadn't stopped the whole time.

'Sweet dreams,' he whispered, then he was gone.

I stayed in my room when he left. I heard him go into the living room and say goodbye to my parents as if nothing had happened. I listened to the sound of my mother trying to make small talk over the muffled hum of the television, her false, tinkly laugh, her voice too loud as she called out, 'Goodbye!' The weird finality of the front door closing behind him, the what now? I could almost feel them – my mother, at least – waiting for me to bound down the stairs all starry-eyed to tell them all about the nice young man who'd come calling. She'd be on the edge of her chair, brittle with expectation.

There was a dizzy sickness, half thrill, half dread, spreading out inside me.

I couldn't go downstairs. Not after what I'd just done. I couldn't stare them in the eyes like nothing had happened. Even I couldn't lie that well. So I stayed in my room, well aware that the curiosity would be too much for my mum, and she'd come up, sooner or later. I lay on my bed, propped up on my elbows with a French book open in front of me, and pinned my eyes to the page, waiting till the waiting got too much for her. I counted time with my heartbeat. It didn't take long before I heard the faint creak of the living room door, and her footsteps on the stairs. I focused on the page, keeping my head empty, blank, my body a still and secret place.

'Well,' she said, after she'd pushed open my door, and stood there for seconds, and I'd failed to look up. It was hot in the room already; it got hotter still with her standing there, staring at me. My head felt like it was burning. I pressed my hands into my cheeks, and stared down into my book.

'He seems like a nice young man,' she went on, and those were exactly the words I knew she'd say, with exactly the same dose of hurt backing them up. *Why haven't you told me about him before?* she meant. *And see, Mrs C was right, there is a young man.*

But every word my mum utters comes with a ladle-load of undercurrents and I learned long ago never to tell her a thing. Not that I'd ever tell her about this, of course. I stared at the page so hard my eyes were popping. I had to speak or I'd never be rid of her.

'He's OK,' I said through the palms of my hands, squashed up against the sides of my mouth. 'But I've got my French. I want to finish it for tomorrow.'

The silence in the room was tangible, agony. I could barely breathe. 'Right,' she said, after an age, in the thinnest of voices. And out she went again, closing the door behind her, so quietly, so dismissed. Still I stayed where I was, rigid, staring at nothing. I couldn't bear to come back into my body, not yet. Eventually I heard the crack as the TV was unplugged, then taps running downstairs, and cups being put away. Lights flicking off, the creak of the stairs. Still I couldn't move; I was suspended, all feeling on hold.

''Night, pet,' my dad said and rapped his fingers on my door on his way past. My mum said nothing, letting me know I'd done her wrong.

If only she knew.

I waited till they were in bed, till the house was silent and I was pretty sure they'd be asleep. Then at last I moved, my arms and legs prickling with pins and needles, life tingling back into my veins. I crept out into the bathroom, and stared at my reflection in the mirror. Dark eyes stared back at me, smudged blacker with day-old khol. I squirted cleanser onto cotton wool and wiped it over my skin, streaking white over white. I searched my face, looking for changes, and found none. Nothing had changed and yet everything had. The eyes staring back at me remained black, huge pupils drowning out the blue. My face gave nothing away. It never does. It is an art, perfected over years. I look at my face I see a stranger, I see nothing. What I am inside: hidden. So deep I wouldn't recognise myself.

I needed a bath, and turned the taps on, just halfway, so the water in the pipes wouldn't wake my parents. I filled the bath barely a quarter full and climbed in. Half-heartedly I splashed the water over my skin, thinking how I could have gone and got myself pregnant. I hadn't given it a thought at the time.

I hadn't thought of anything, except the thrill of it all. The *go on*. The *what if*.

I pulled out the plug and stared down at myself, strangely detached, as the water ran away. My mother is always telling me I'm distant and cold, and she's right, but I've had to be like that, just to stop myself being swallowed up.

I stepped out of the bath and let the cool air rush goosepimples over my skin. Still damp, I tiptoed back to my room, and slid into bed. Against my skin the sheets were still warm; I could feel where Danny had lain, the heat off his skin. I pressed my body into the warmth, and I could smell him, on my pillow.

And all night I lay there, breathing him in, thinking, what have I done? Round and round my head it went: oh God, what have we done?

I didn't want to sleep. I didn't want to block out the feeling.

We'd made it real, Danny and me. We'd made it forever.

4

I did sleep, eventually, but not much and I woke up feeling sick and punched out, from tiredness, from the *thrill* of it. I combed my hair in the little mirror over my chest of drawers, I drew khol around my eyes, blackening them up.

This morning I did look different. I looked pale, I looked tired. And I looked dark in the eyes. *Dead* dark.

I used to think I was ugly. When I was little my mum used to force a brush through my hair every morning till my neck ached from being yanked backwards; she'd have the length of my hair in one hand and the brush in the other and she'd pair them up against each other like it was a fight. She'd grit her teeth, nostrils flaring, her and the hairbrush, against me. But the hairbrush only ever cut the surface, and tears would back up in my eyes from the pain, and the shame. Then when I couldn't stand it any more she'd drop the brush and flick the band down off her wrist, over her fingers and into my hair, trapping it. 'You've got hair like my father,' she'd say, like it was some crime. And she'd stare at my head, frowning, as tendrils and curls broke out of the band, springing up again, free. She'd sigh, then, defeated for another day, and home her disappointment in on my face instead. 'Oh, freckles,' she'd mutter, chewing on the side of her lip. 'Oh, well. Maybe you'll grow out of them.'

I hated my wild, dark hair, and my freckles. I wanted to be like the other girls at school; princess-blonde and shiny. And I hated being tall, and thin. 'Louise is a beanpole,' my mum would say to neighbours, to shop assistants, to strangers in the street, and I'd stand there, mortified, trying to be smaller. 'A long streak of nothing.'

Nothing.

But then things started changing, around Year Eight. I stopped growing upwards, and my stick-thin arms and legs filled out a little. Then the freckles started fading, and by the time I was thirteen they'd disappeared all together. I got my hair cut up to my shoulders in a bob and let the curls just be themselves, and suddenly all those flat-haired Barbie clones were tweaking at my ringlets saying, 'God, you're so lucky, my hair won't do a thing except hang.' And, 'What I'd give to have hair like yours.'

It was weird, believe me, having those girls envying me.

Weirder still to have the boys suddenly hanging around. Jacob fancied me, I knew he did. And Miles.

And others too, if I'm honest. But to me it seemed so surreal. It was like they fancied some faint, artificial image of me, not the real thing.

Whenever I looked in the mirror I saw the gawky Louise with the skinny legs and the frizzy hair; I felt like her still, inside. I felt like that every time my mother looked at me, with that wistful, critical look on her face.

No one ever looked, and saw, and liked the real me, freckles or no freckles. No one, except Danny.

Heat rushed up into my head. Danny saw me. Danny knew me, like nobody else ever had.

My mum was in the kitchen, as usual. Waiting for me. Waiting a little more actively than usual, since there was something going on, a boy on the scene, and all that. My mum always longs for something to be going on. Most of the time there is nothing, so she has to make it up; 'So-and-so's not been around much, she was looking tired last times I saw her, do you suppose something's wrong? Mrs Thingy said they're knocking the old church hall down and putting up flats, well I can tell you they'll have to knock me down too before they get away with that. I saw Mrs Whatsit in the High Street today, and do you know what? She blanked me. Totally. Like she hadn't even seen I was there.'

It would never occur to my mum that maybe Mrs

Whatsit genuinely hadn't seen her. Oh no. There is a drama manifesting itself every two seconds in my mother's kitchen-table world.

She was sitting at the table now in her dressing-gown, toying with a cup of tea. She'd have been there since my dad left for work, at least half an hour before. I tried not to look at her, though I could feel her staring at me. Sometimes I wished that just now and again I could come down in the morning and she wouldn't be there. I didn't want her dead or anything – I didn't want her *gone* – I just didn't want her to *always* be there, just waiting. I wished she had something else to do instead of sitting there in that tatty dressing-gown, surrounded by all the stupid gadgets in the kitchen that she keeps on buying because she seems to think they'll make a difference, somehow – the blender, the bread-maker, the electric can opener and the juicer, all cluttering up the place and turning slowly yellow, from lack of use.

I picked up the kettle and shook it. It was full of water of course, and hot, just boiled, but I flicked the switch back on anyway. I could feel my mum watching me, I could hear the words, fighting to come out, *The kettle's just boiled, Louise, you don't need to put it on again.*

She said nothing. Now I knew she was hyped up for the bigger picture. I could feel her eyes on my back, waiting. She'd have to speak first; I never did. But she was putting me off, watching me like that. I took a cup off the draining board and opened the cupboard above the kettle to take a tea bag out of the box, remembering just too late to hold my breath, and the awful smell of old flour hit me. That smell can turn my stomach and sicken my head like nothing on earth. It's always instant this and instant that. My mother's cupboards are stuffed with packets of everything imaginable. Instant soup, instant cake mix, white sauce, cheese sauce, antique dried out curry-mix . . . *a meal in a minute – just add water* . . . all crammed in together and most of them long past their sell-by dates.

They've all been there forever. For as long as *I* can remember.

I plopped the tea bag into the cup, poured on the water, stirred it about with a spoon, and stood there, letting it stew. And I picked at the mat under the kettle with my fingernail, playing for time. The mat had been there forever, too, like everything else in the kitchen, apart from the kettle. They'd bought the mat because the old kettle didn't switch itself off in time and used to spit hot bubbles of water from its spout when it started to boil. I remember that old kettle. I remember watching it hiss and scream, ready to explode. And I remember all those other gadgets when they were still bright and white and packed with promise. It was like she'd bought up a job lot, everything the good wife and mother needs. Before the disappointment set in.

I wondered how long she could sit there, sipping at that tea, and watching me. She'd probably put gin in her cup. I knew I would, if I ever ended up like her.

'Well then,' she said at last, in that over-bright tone that let me know that yes, I had hurt her yet again but she'd decided not to dwell on it. *She* was making an effort.

I squeezed the tea bag against the spoon with my finger, feeling the heat sting into my skin, and recede. Still I delayed turning round. I couldn't think what to say. I wasn't going to tell her anything *real*, of course. I'd tell her what she wanted to hear, if I ever knew what that was.

'I hoped you might be feeling a little more communicative this morning,' she said, her voice slipping from brightness to a semi-whisper. I dropped the tea bag into the bin under the sink, and then hesitated. I needed to get the milk, but the fridge was on the other side of the room.

'I do have a right to know what's going on.' I heard the scrape of the chair as she stood up, and the thin edge of a performance, spiking up.

Carefully I turned around. I focused on the front of her dressing-gown, avoiding her eye. She'd got a stain down the front there. Yoghurt or something, greasy and pale. That stain repulsed me, making it easier to lie.

'Nothing's going on.'

'It's not every day that we have a young man calling to see you.' She'd flipped back to the falsely bright again. It was always like this; if you mapped out the changes in her voice you'd get a pattern. You'd get a web.

'Danny's just a friend,' I muttered to that stain, and, bizarrely, that must have been the right thing to say. She smiled, and the shock of it caught my eye, had me looking her in the face. Her eyes were bright, too bright, in her pale, wiped-out face.

'I do remember what it's like to be young,' she confided, way too excited. She raised her hands as if to touch me and panic had me turning back to the sink, pouring my tea away. Forced, shared intimacies were the worst and I wanted to get out.

'I've got to get my stuff,' I blurted. 'Don't want to be late.' And I bolted back upstairs to get my bag, leaving her there, arms outstretched, with no audience. I wished I'd skipped the whole kitchen bit altogether.

I grabbed up my stuff as fast as I could, but there she was, just coming out of the kitchen and into the hall as I ran downstairs again.

'What about breakfast?' she started, but I didn't stop.

'Not hungry,' I said and then I was out of the front door, down the path and away from her. Immediately, I felt the oppression lifting. Fleetingly I wondered how many more cups of tea it would take for my mother to go and change out of that hideous dressing-gown and into some clothes and get on with whatever it was that she did all day to keep herself so bored. But then I took a few steps more, turned the corner, and forgot about her altogether.

I wanted to be on time to meet Danny, but little coils of embarrassment were setting themselves loose inside me as I walked up towards the main road. I didn't know what I was going to say to him. I didn't know what *he'd* say.

It had all happened so suddenly. So one minute you're one thing, the next you're another. So real and yet so unreal, like a dream. Blink your eyes for a second and it hadn't happened, almost.

He wasn't there.

I waited for a while, looking up his road. I waited, trying to look like I wasn't waiting. I walked on past his road, I turned and walked back on myself, and walked past his road again. You could see a long way up that road if you stared hard enough, past all the houses, till they got smaller and smaller, blurring out of sight.

He wasn't coming. It was half-past eight and it had

been twenty past when I got here. He wasn't coming and I didn't know what I felt the most; disappointed or just plain embarrassed. I walked on to school on my own, feeling strangely disjointed. I kept expecting him to run up behind me, catching me up, but he didn't. I expected it so much that my neck ached from the determination not to turn around, and see.

Maybe he'd just wanted to get what he could out of me, and how pleased he'd be now, that he'd got the lot. Maybe he'd tell everyone. Well if he did I'd just deny it. No one would believe him.

Yet somehow I didn't think he was like that.

Cara was standing by the traffic lights, just about to go on ahead without me. Meeting her was like the cut off; I knew I wouldn't see Danny now. But even so as I looked around to cross the road I still turned and glanced behind me, just in case.

'You're late,' Cara said. 'I was going to go without you.' And then she was straight off into some *should I/ shouldn't I?* about James Clark and Alex Nicholson and God knows who else, and what about her denim skirt, did it look all right with her black boots or did she really need to get brown? And I walked beside her, listening to all that crap like I always did but I kept getting the weird feeling that though I hadn't seen him Danny was behind me, watching me, following me. I felt it so much there were prickles creeping up under my hair. I tried not to turn my head but I couldn't help myself.

'What are you looking at?' Cara snapped, and she looked back too. If he had been there he disappeared pretty quickly then. I didn't see him, and Cara certainly didn't. She screwed up her eyes at me, pissed off that I hadn't been hanging off her every word. 'Emma thinks the black ones look good, if I wear patterned tights,' she said, letting me know that Emma would never let anything distract *her* from Cara's dilemmas.

I shuffled into school and into tutorial, and sat next to Cara with this great secret hidden inside me. It amazed me that she could be so oblivious. You'd think it would be written all over me, what I'd done. You'd think people would see, just by looking at me. I walked from class to class, from one block to another, feeling like I was naked, transparent, like everyone would see right into me if they looked.

There was a girl in the year above me called Lisa Morton who we all knew had done it. It was hot news way back, at the start of last year when I still thought everyone was a virgin till they'd at least left school. Lisa Morton did it at a party with some guy in her year. Monday morning it was all round the school, how she'd got off with this guy and done it with him, right there on the living room floor in front of everyone else. People were standing round, chanting and throwing beer cans at them. Cara and I couldn't believe it when we heard. I mean, how could anyone do that? Cara and I didn't even know who Lisa Morton was but Emma did; she said she lived in Cranfield same as her, and came in on the bus. So the three of us stalked her out, wanting to get a good look at someone who'd done it. We expected her legs to be bowed or something; not meeting at the top.

'There she is,' Emma hissed and we ducked down behind the bunker that hid the bins at the back of the canteen, and peered round as two girls walked by. 'Tall one,' Emma whispered.

She wasn't bow-legged, or hunched over, or even limping. She didn't even look ashamed or embarrassed, and you'd think she would after all the things everyone was saying about her. You'd think she'd look like she wanted to die but she didn't. She did look like a total slapper, though, with home-dyed hair gone black at the roots and that vacant look in her eyes that thick girls put there to make themselves look hard. She looked like someone who'd do it.

You wouldn't say the same about me.

I could almost blank it out, pretend it hadn't happened. Almost.

At lunch I met up with Cara and Emma and we wandered across the main playground and sat on the strip of grass that ran alongside the wall separating the school from the old people's home next door. We had a full view of the playground from there.

'Let's observe,' Cara said, and the two of them sat watching the boys across the playground, coming in and out the gates or just hanging around, while I squinted into the sun, searching for Danny. He wasn't there.

'Andrew Jones,' Cara said.

'Mmmn, nice bum,' Emma said. 'Nine out of ten. Stephen Ross.'

'Eight and a half. Bit spotty.' Cara jogged me with her elbow. 'Your turn,' she said.

'What?'

'We're doing Year Elevens,' she said, speaking loud like I was deaf or just plain stupid. 'Marks out of ten. It's your turn.'

'Oh I don't know. Andrew Jones.'

'I've just done him,' Cara snapped, and I stopped watching the gates just long enough to see Cara and Emma look at each other, and boy was that look loaded.

'Look count me out,' I said. 'I've got a headache.'

Cara shrugged like she didn't believe me and no doubt they'd be talking about me later but I couldn't be bothered to care. I did have a headache suddenly. I closed my eyes and dipped my head onto my knees just to get my face out the sun.

I wasn't going to see Danny now. There was no point in even looking any more.

Then in the afternoon I'd just split from Cara and was on my way to art when Danny's mate Richard caught up with me in the corridor.

'Louise,' he called behind me, in a half-whisper, stopping me. He was a short guy, Richard, with longish dark hair, falling in his face. He always wore an old, black leather jacket; all Danny's mates did. 'I've got this for you,' he said and handed me a piece of paper, folded over and over into a tiny square. 'From Danny.'

I took the note, and I wondered what he knew about me, and Danny. I half expected him to smirk, or make some comment or at least give me a knowing look. But he didn't. He just stood there, while everyone else in the corridor dispersed.

'Read it,' he said, and waited like a messenger boy while I unfolded it. Danny's writing was oversized and leaning to the right, scrawled across the page.

Dear Louise
I need to see you. Richard knows where I am. Meet him
this afternoon, after school. He'll bring you to me.
If you don't come, I'll understand.
D

So cryptic. Like the drama was all-important. I could feel it, pulling me in.

I stared at the note, not sure how to react.

'Well?' Richard said, after a while. He obviously knew what was in the note. He probably knew everything else, too.

Suddenly I felt tears stinging my eyes; I don't know why. Sometimes I think it's just the easy route out, a few tears. Sometimes it's just what's expected.

It seemed to be the right response, now. Richard put his hand on my arm. 'You'll be OK,' he said, gently. 'I'll meet you at the gates. Don't worry.'

I kept the note secret from Cara. God knows what she'd say if she saw it. God knows what she'd say if she knew what I'd done. Meeting Richard at three-thirty without her knowing was easy enough. It was Wednesday, we had French last thing and Cara went straight from French to Orchestra Practice. Danny would have known that, of course. If he'd planned all this, he'd planned it well.

Richard was waiting just outside the school gates. He'd got a cigarette cupped in his hand, half tucked up the sleeve of his jacket. He took a long drag through his fingers when he saw me, then flicked the butt out into the street.

'All right?' he said through his hair, then he started walking, towards the alleyway up the side of the school. He led me towards the footbridge over the motorway, but instead of going over it we went down the side, to where there was just bushes and trees, between the motorway itself and the council estate. I didn't even know you could get down there. I listened to the roar of the cars and to my heart, starting up a hard, nervous march.

We walked a long way into the trees, till we were right near the high-boarded fence that ran along the edge of the motorway, put up to try to dim the noise from the cars. Danny was sitting on the horizontal base of a fallen tree. He had his back to us and he couldn't have heard us approach over the endless scream of the motorway yet somehow he knew we were there, I was sure he did. He was sitting with one leg raised up, knee bent, and he had his hand draped around his knee, toying with a cigarette. The trees were thick around him, closing a roof above his head but there was one gap, made bigger as the wind rustled the leaves, and the sunlight cut through, lighting him up.

'Danny?' I felt really nervous for some reason, maybe because of last night, maybe just because of the weirdness of meeting him like this. And I wished Richard would go away and not just stand there, like he was on guard duty.

Slowly Danny lowered his leg, dropped his cigarette and ground it out with his foot. Then he stood up, and turned around, and then I realised why Richard was there; he was the audience. It was all so staged, everything. It was like I'd walked into a film, into Danny's own made-up story, and I was part of it. I was part of his escape.

'I wasn't sure you'd come,' Danny said, sounding like *he* was nervous too. He walked right up to me and took hold of my hands, and we stood there, just holding hands, so innocent, after last night.

'You didn't go to school,' I said. 'I didn't know what to think.'

'I didn't know what to think either,' Danny said, and he kind of laughed, mouth tilted up one side into half a smile. I wanted to kiss him. He held onto my hands, tight and I clutched back, fingers busy, busy, holding on. 'I didn't want to be at school. I didn't want to have other people getting in the way. Messing things up. This is so special,' he said. 'You're so special.' I watched his mouth as he spoke; I wanted to see those words as well as hear them; that way I'd remember them, always. 'I love you,' he said, and my heart was thumping, thumping.

'I love you too,' I said, all in a rush.

A twig behind me snapped. Richard; I'd forgotten he was there. Danny glanced up, over my shoulder. 'You can go, now,' he said. 'Thanks.' And like a lacky Richard disappeared, dismissed. How weird was that? Only I didn't think of it at the time. I didn't think of anything except that Danny had said he loved me.

He said it again. 'I've fancied you for years,' he said, and I wanted to hear more. 'You used to wear your socks rolled down to your shoes.'

I laughed. 'Not since I was about twelve.'

'And you used to go about with that girl from Fairview Drive. Natalie Banks.'

I wasn't laughing now. A cold hand flicked a chill up under my hair. 'How did you know Natalie?'

'From Juniors,' he said, like it was the most obvious thing. I couldn't even remember Danny being at my junior school. I had the strangest feeling of my head splitting in two, looking back and looking forward at the same time.

We went and sat down on that fallen-down tree, and he kissed me then for a long, long time. Even the roar of the motorway seemed romantic, somehow.

'Give me your phone,' Danny said and I did, and he put in his number, but he didn't put it under his name. He wanted us to stay secret, *special*, so he put it in under YAMIE. Then he did the same with my number, in his. *You And Me In Eternity.*

His number's still in my phone. I've even pressed it

once or twice, though I've always hung up again, before it's started to ring.

'I want you to have this,' he said, and he wriggled off his finger a silver ring, thick and way too big for me but he took hold of my hand and put it on my finger anyway. My *wedding* finger, if you believe in all that stuff.

'This is forever, you know,' he said and I did know it. 'There's no going back.'

It was a thick, snake-shaped ring, curling round so that the head and the tail met and joined. I slipped it into my pocket before I got home, and kept it there while my mum jumped up from the table where she'd been waiting for me, and fussed and poured tea and complained and asked questions and generally did my head in with the insufferable blanket of claustrophobia that she'd have me suffocated with, eventually.

He did plan it well. The next day was Thursday. Athletics after school, easily missed. Danny waited for me, just past the gates, after everyone else had gone on, and I walked back with him to his house. His mum was out, taking his sister to ballet, and I had a whole hour, before I needed to be home.

This time I lay back on his bed while he unwrapped me like a present. He kissed every centimetre of me, from left to right, top to toe. Again I was shaking, but from all things good this time, no fear, no more what-ifs. He kissed me all over and then he sat back, and just looked at me. 'You are so beautiful,' he said, and I'll never forget the look in his eyes. 'I want to remember you, every little bit of you; I want you in my head, forever.'

I lay there naked, shaking, while he stared at me like he wanted to stare at me forever. Then he reached down beside his bed and came back up with a packet of condoms.

'Best to be prepared this time,' he said, and then I knew he hadn't planned it the other night. I knew it had just happened; that it was meant to be. It was out of his control. Out of our control. It was pure, real, what we had. There was some greater force than us, driving us.

How could it ever be wrong, what we did?

He loved me. He told me so, over and over. He kissed me like he needed me, just to stay alive. He held me like he might die, if ever he let me go.

Later, I sat at the table eating green beans and some strange pie filled with blue cheese, apple and spinach. My mother sat at one end of the table, my father at the other, and I occupied the midway position along one side, with the wall as my opposite companion. A few months ago I'd stopped eating meat so my mother was attacking vegetarian recipes like we were all on a mission. I'd have been happy with a lump of cheese. Still, the strange taste of the pie distracted me from the chill wind that blew across the table from north to south and south to north.

My, what a chilly wind.

I listened to the sound of steel cutlery on china, trying to find a tune in there somewhere. And I stared down at my plate and up at the wall, determined not to turn to the left or the right, and see their miserable faces.

'This is nice,' my dad said at last, like he didn't much mean it.

'It would have been nicer half an hour ago. When it was ready.'

'It's not my fault the traffic was bad.' My dad spoke slowly to her, like she was a child.

'It's not my fault either,' my mum snapped back. She was tapping her fork against the side of her plate, ratter, tatter, tatter. 'And it's not my fault that the dinner's spoiled.'

'It isn't spoiled. It's very nice.' He took a few more mouthfuls to prove it. 'Is it something new?'

'Yes. It's vegetarian. I thought Louise would like it.'

'I do,' I said, automatically.

'You'd have liked it a lot more half an hour ago.'

And so it went on, this happy family meal, much like it did every night, with small variations. Words bounced back and forth, occasionally hitting me, though I tried to just bat them away.

Sometimes I looked at my mum and dad and wondered why on earth they ever got together in the first place, never mind why they then hung around so long, trying to have me.

I looked at their pissed-off faces and I wondered, were they ever happy? Did they ever hold each other like they really meant it, loose limbed and unencumbered? Did they ever *laugh*?

I couldn't imagine it. I couldn't imagine them ever being like Danny and me. Doing the things we do. It wasn't the same. It wasn't anything like the same.

We'd never end up like them. I thought. *I'd die first.*

I stopped going to athletics after that, and went back to Danny's on Thursdays instead. There were only four weeks till the end of term; no one would notice.

I told my mum that Danny was a runner too. I wouldn't have told her anything at all if I could have helped it but she couldn't stop herself from prying. A whole week of mulling it over to herself was too much for her.

'Have you seen that young man?' she asked, trying

to sound all nonchalant, though she probably hadn't thought about anything else all week. She'd got a recipe book open on the side and was weighing stuff on her new digital scales, though she didn't have a clue how they worked. It was guesswork. Bad guesswork. She'd got flour spilt all over her bare feet. She was wearing her dressing-gown, at getting on for five o'clock. I wondered if she'd been wearing it all day, and the thought sickened me.

'What young man?' I asked, just to annoy her.

'You know what young man, Louise,' she snapped. I watched the colour flash red up her face. She still managed to stop herself from looking at me, though, busy as she was with those scales.

'Yes,' I said.

'Yes, what?'

'Yes I've seen him.'

'When?' She turned her head, moving quickly, and a rain of flour wafted down across the floor.

'Just now.'

'What do you mean?' she gasped, all in a rush. She stood there staring at me, flour packet in one hand, oversized spoon in the other.

'At athletics,' I lied. 'He's a runner.' I forced myself to meet her eye. She had a flour streak on her face and her forehead was all shiny. She looked pathetic. 'We're going to go running together,' I said, as soon as the idea came to me, and what a brilliant idea it was. 'In the evenings, sometimes. When it's cooled down. I need to practise more and if he comes with me it's safer, isn't it?'

'Yes, of course,' she said, because she couldn't argue with that, could she? She smiled at me, though there was a frown above her eyes still, and a nerve twitching in her cheek.

I made myself smile back.

Lying to my mum was second nature. It was easy. Sometimes it was a pleasure. I did it just to keep her out.

Danny laughed when I told him. I knew he would. He wrapped his arms around me and squeezed me tight, and laughed into my hair.

'Mmm. Can't wait,' he said. 'You look so sexy in your running shorts.'

He turned up at my house in his football shorts and a T-shirt. He actually jogged on the spot on the doorstep when my dad answered the door, and carried on jogging, and making inane chat about the importance of warming up beforehand, while I laced up my trainers.

We ran to the river at the far end of the park. No one could see us there, hidden by the trees.

'God, you're unfit,' I laughed as Danny flopped back,

down into the grass. I lay down beside him, leaning over him. He grabbed me and pulled me down to kiss me but he was so puffed he started coughing, and then laughing, and coughing some more.

'Listen to you!' I pulled away from him, and lay down on my back, star-fished. The grass was cool under my limbs, pressing criss-crosses into my skin.

'I've got something for us,' Danny said when at last he got his breath back. He'd got his cigarettes stuffed in the pocket of his shorts. There were only a couple of cigarettes in the packet, and some Rizla papers, and stuck further down a little brown cube, wrapped in cling film. He hooked it out with his finger, and squashed it a little, against his thumb.

'Yum, yum,' he said, and I met his eyes, and laughed.

He sat up, and laid out a Rizla paper on his thigh. He split open a cigarette and sprinkled its insides onto the paper, and crumbled the dope on top of that. It looked like a stock cube, like the ones my gran used to make gravy. Then he passed me the cigarette packet.

'Tear off the inside of the lid,' he said, 'and roll it up, but not too tight.' So I did, and then he said, 'You've done this before,' though I hadn't, of course.

He tucked the roach into the end with fingers so steady and exact that he should have been an artist. He held the spliff between his lips, cupped one hand around the end while he struck up his lighter with the other, took three sharp drags in a row, then passed it to me.

It was a ritual, the first of many.

We went back to my house, for a drink.

We'd run all the way and I'd stared up at the sky as I ran, head back, feeling like I was rushing through space. I felt so free, like nothing on earth. I could see the stars jumping out in the purple end-of-day sky; they popped in my eyes as I stared, wide, unblinking.

Danny held me by the hand. We stopped outside my house to get our breath. There was a parachute inside my head, floating slowly down. I didn't want it to come down; I laughed out loud, sending it back up again, and clamped my free hand over my mouth.

'Shh!' I said to Danny, even though it was me who'd laughed. I peered into his eyes. His pupils were huge and black, like alleyways; I could see myself running down them.

We walked steadily, carefully up to the back door. I concentrated hard on the ground, willing it to keep still.

No one was in the kitchen, but Danny let the door slam shut behind us and instantly my mum came scuttling down the hall.

'We've come back for a drink,' I said. 'We're hot.' My voice was too loud, and I had to stop myself from giggling.

'Yes,' my mum said. 'You look a little flushed.' She was looking at me curiously so I switched my gaze down a notch, away from her face. She was wearing a silky blouse with little flowers on it; I tried to focus on the flowers but they seemed to be waving around. 'Well,' she said uncertainly. 'There's some orange juice in the fridge. Don't be long now.' And off she went again, back to my dad.

'Hello, Mrs Osborne,' Danny called after her, a little too late.

He kissed me goodbye at the back door, kissed me long and slow, holding me so close to him. I could feel the flutter of his eyelashes against my cheek as he pressed his face against mine, and the warmth of his body through the soft cotton of his T-shirt. Kissing wasn't enough; it never was. I wanted to drown in him.

When he left I ran upstairs and watched him walking away, from my window. Just before he got out of view he stopped and looked up, as if he'd been able to sense me there, watching him. Even from that distance I could see his eyes. He raised a hand; he smiled.

I'll never forget how he looked, then, smiling up at me. It's stamped in my head, indelible.

5

It was Wednesday; when school finished Cara went straight off to Orchestra, and I went off to meet Danny outside the school gates and walk back with him, secretly of course. But I was just heading out the playground when I heard Cara running up behind me.

'Louise!' she called, catching me up. 'Orchestra's cancelled. I can come back to your house instead. See what you're wearing to the concert. Grab this—' She shoved her clarinet box at me and started digging around in her bag for her phone. 'I'll just text my mum; she won't mind.'

I caught hold of the clarinet and my stomach did a slow, halfway turn. Danny would be outside the gates, waiting for me.

'There's not much point,' I said, playing for time. 'I haven't even thought about what to wear yet.'

'All the more reason you need me!' Cara said, pushing her bag back over her shoulder. And then she was head down, busy with her phone. She didn't see Danny as we walked past him, but I did.

He was on the other side of the road, leaning against

the wall of a house where the alleyway started. I shot him a glance that I hoped told him *sorry, but what can I do? I'd much rather be with you.* But by the look on his face he didn't read it that way.

Suddenly I wished it didn't all have to be such a big secret.

Cara threw herself down onto my bed, totally at home.

'I haven't been here for ages,' she complained. 'I can't even remember what you've got inside your wardrobe.'

'Nothing much,' I said, sitting on the end of my bed, right by her feet. 'Nothing new, anyway.'

Suddenly she sat up. 'I want to borrow your blue shirt. I'm wearing my jeans and my new boots and it'll go perfectly.' She stood up, opened my wardrobe and started furrowing. I lay back and watched her. 'I'll take it now,' she said, yanking it off the hanger, and then, as an afterthought, 'You weren't going to wear it, were you?'

'Probably not. I might wear my black skirt and top.'

'What, this one?' she asked anxiously, pulling out my skirt and holding it against herself. 'Do you think I should wear a skirt too, then?'

Without waiting for a reply she sat down on the bed beside me, with my skirt and blue shirt on her lap and said, 'I'm thinking of getting a fringe cut. What do you think?' There was a big mirror on the wall opposite my bed, and she leaned forward slightly to stare at herself, and started playing with her hair. I sat up beside her, right up close so we both fitted into the mirror. There we were, one dark, one blonde. Cara smiled, more at herself than at me. She knew she looked good.

Still, not everyone liked long, blonde hair. Danny liked hair like mine that you could push your hand into and get it stuck; he loved the way the roots tightened themselves around his fingers. And he loved my bones, too, the thin ones just below my throat. He said they were so delicate he could snap them between two fingers if he wanted to; said they were like butterfly wings and he liked to trace the rim from the top of my breast bone and up and out into my shoulders. *Look*, he said once, *I can hook my fingers right round your neck . . .*

'No fringe,' I said and Cara twisted her nose, considering. She tipped her head forward, pulling strands of hair down over her face.

'What about layers, then, round the sides?'

'What about me?' I said. 'Maybe I should go blonde.' And I grabbed great handfuls of her hair, draping it around my face, to see how it would look. She'd got her face up against mine now, screaming with laughter; I could feel her breath on my cheek.

65

'My God, you look like a witch!' she screeched in my ear.

Against the yellow of her hair my olive skin looked positively green. I got hold of more of her hair; poor Cara was neck-bent, contorted as I pulled her hair and spread it out over mine. We were both killing ourselves laughing. I couldn't believe how awful I looked. Like I'd been dead for about a year.

'Here,' I said. 'Lets finish me off.' I rummaged in my make-up bag for my eye liner, leaning forward and so freeing Cara, who crooked her head from side to side, rubbing her neck. Her hair started to fall away from me; with one hand I grabbed it back, laying it across the top of my head. With the other hand I drew thick black lines around my eyes, way off my lashes; I filled the gaps in till there was just so much black. I looked straight out of a horror movie.

'Now me,' Cara said, taking the pencil. She drew herself some Cleopatra eyes, sweeping right up at the edges, way over the top. Then we sat there, staring at each other in the mirror. We both have blue eyes but Cara's are baby-pale, and mine are dark, with black rings around the irises, darkening them still more. 'I was wondering what you think about Jacob,' she said suddenly, like it had been on her mind for a while. 'Only you don't seem that interested in him any more.'

Cara's face was flushed, pink splashes on her white cheeks, and her eyes were mega-bright. I knew she fancied Jacob. And I never had, not really. I'd never really fancied anyone, till Danny. I had to tell her. I *had* to.

'Jacob's really nice,' I said, trying to pick my words, 'but I'm sure he likes you as much as me. And anyway –' I couldn't think how to put it and in the end I just blurted it out '– I'm kind of seeing someone else.'

'Who?' Cara gawped at me, the curiosity on her face battling with disbelief. Already I wished I hadn't said anything.

'Danny,' I said, and my heart was pounding.

'Danny?' she repeated, like I'd said something ridiculous. 'Danny *Fisher*? You're not,' she stated. 'You told me it was nothing.' She turned away from the mirror now and stared at me for real; I stared back and saw everything she thought of me, and of Danny, cross her eyes.

I found myself needing to make excuses, not really because I thought there was anything wrong with Danny – I just felt like I needed to defend him. 'He's really sweet when you get to know him,' I said, almost like it was an apology. 'And he really likes me.'

Cara carried on staring at me, unconvinced. Then she turned her gaze back to the mirror and I did the same; it put a little distance back in between us. Why did I have to explain myself to her, or to anyone for that matter? I could feel myself getting irritated, with Cara, with myself. Danny was right; it was other people that fucked things up.

'How long has this been going on?' Cara asked, sounding very much like my mother. Now I felt really annoyed. What had it got to do with her anyway?

Still I toned things down a bit. 'Not long. A week or two.' Cara's eyes narrowed in the mirror; God, she could look haughty. 'It probably won't come to anything. I've only seen him a couple of times.' I shrugged my shoulders dismissively, hating myself for lying.

'Well at least that leaves Jacob free for me,' Cara said, and she was looking at herself again now, examining her skin. I took that to mean I was forgiven, for my secrets, if not my bad taste. Suddenly she remembered something; and she bounced round on the bed to face me, mouth and eyes popping right open. 'Guess what! You know Clare Minty and Ned Samuels got off together at Nicky Turner's party? Well they actually *did it*! At the party! Clare told Emma in Spanish. Can you believe it?' She screwed up her face in disgust. 'What a dog!'

Cara didn't need a response. Gossip spread, she went back to her reflection. I watched her fiddling with her hair and I just thanked God that I hadn't told her that *I'd* done it, with Danny. Or she'd be calling me a dog too, or thinking it at least. I wished I hadn't told her anything. I wished we could just keep it secret forever, Danny and me. But you can't live like that. You can't live two lives.

Danny was totally pissed off that I'd told Cara.

We'd gone to the boathouse the next day after school. It had started to rain on the way, fat, heavy drops thumping onto our shoulders and heads and into our eyes as we ran across the grounds of the old house, and into the cover of the trees.

We were inside the boathouse now, listening to the rain pummelling the broken roof like stones and streaming down through the gaps. Here and there it hit straight through both the roof and the slats below, stinging the water underneath with a ping. It was a precarious place to shelter but somehow that made it all the more special, and we huddled together in the one dry corner, with the rain dripping all around us. I wished it could be like that forever, just me and Danny and no one else. Just us, dipped out of time.

He had his arm around me. There was nothing to do in the rain except kiss and talk and smoke. I had this rope of sadness, tugging away at me inside. I felt like I'd betrayed him by telling Cara; I knew he'd mind but I'd had no idea how much.

'I had to tell her,' I said. 'She's my best friend. She was going on about Jacob Warren; she fancies him but she didn't want to go after him because she thought I fancied him.'

'Do you?'

'Of course not. That's why I had to tell her about you. Don't you see?'

But he didn't see. All he could see was that I might fancy Jacob Warren and that I'd been discussing him with Cara.

He was holding me up against him; with the fingers of the other hand he was tracing the lines of my ribs through my shirt. Slowly that hand stilled, and drew away. 'Jacob Warren fancies you,' he said and I felt these walls of frustration slamming in on me. This wasn't about Jacob Warren; couldn't he see that? This was about me, and him; no one else mattered unless we *let* them matter.

'You shouldn't have told her,' Danny said, sitting up and using the hand that had been on my ribs to dig his cigarettes and lighter out from his back pocket. He took his arm away from my shoulder too now, and lit up. One for me, one for him. I didn't want a cigarette right then but I took it anyway.

'But why not?' I held my cigarette out between my fingers and a rain drop hit it, smack, right by the nib. 'Why shouldn't I tell her? Why shouldn't we tell everyone? *Why* does it all have to be so secret?'

'What we had these last few weeks is special,' Danny said, and I had the feeling he was talking to himself rather than me. 'I just don't want it to change.'

'It won't change.'

'It will.' He flicked out his hand and the ash flew off his cigarette, scattering across his knee. 'I don't want other people . . . fucking it up.'

'We won't let them,' I said. Sometimes with Danny you could actually see his mood descend, like a cloud coming down. I saw it now, a blackness sinking into him.

'I love you,' he said. 'I don't want anyone trying to take you away from me.'

But Danny was right. Things did start to change.

Cara didn't wait for me in the mornings any more. Sometimes I saw her up ahead, walking on without even looking to see if I was coming. Even on days when I was on my own, without Danny. One day she was up ahead of me; I was walking fast to try and catch her up when a car pulled up alongside her, and Emma got out. She stuck her arm straight through Cara's and they walked on, huddled together. I could hear them laughing, and I held back. I felt I'd lost my place, now, somehow.

On the days that Danny did walk to school with me he kept his arm clamped around my shoulder until we were right in the playground. It was like now that it was out that we were seeing each other he wanted to make sure everyone knew. He was marking me out, staking his claim. Of course I liked it that he loved me, but what he was saying to everyone else was *keep off.*

Cara stopped seeking me out at lunchtime. Sometimes I went to the rec with her, sometimes I didn't. She didn't seem to be bothered either way; after all, Emma was always there.

If I didn't go with Cara at lunch, it was because I was with Danny. If he was around at lunchtime he'd usually want me with him, but often I wouldn't know that until the last minute. It got me down a bit; sometimes I'd want to just go off with Cara and Emma and be like we used to be. Sometimes I didn't want to be dangling on strings.

One morning Danny didn't show up but I knew he was in school later because I saw him, at break, hanging around by the water fountains, with his mates. He made no effort to find me, and speak to me. Emma was off sick, and Cara and I had PE before lunch; we were having such a laugh out on the sports field, alternating between long jump and high jump. We were both pretty useless at high jump; Cara knocked the bar off every time and the only way I could get over was by hurling myself up backwards. Running is one thing, high jump quite another. We were late getting changed for lunch, then we headed off to the rec, automatically, just like we used to.

We sat on a bench near the swings. It was a really hot day and loads of people from school were in the rec. I'd missed this lately, and though I loved Danny and wanted to be with him, it was so nice just being back how I used to be, with my friends, like in the days *before* Danny. Jacob and Miles and some of the other boys from our form wandered into the park, there was a whole crowd of us around that bench. I knew how Cara felt about Jacob so I kind of held back, but I was enjoying all of us just being together, having a laugh. With Danny things were so intense, so isolating.

And I guess I just got carried away. I mean, I didn't think I was flirting, but I guess that's how it looked to Danny.

He was on the other side of the park. I don't know how long he'd been there but suddenly I saw him, with Richard, right over the other side of the football pitch. He was just standing there, staring at me. Miles had been saying something; I'd been listening, I'd been about to say something back but I forgot what, suddenly. I saw Danny and couldn't tear myself away from his stare. My heart flipped out an extra beat. I told myself I was glad just to see him but it felt more like fear, caught-in-the-act fear. Sometimes when Danny looked at me I felt myself move away inside to a different place, a place where there was just me and him.

For a moment I thought he'd come over and join us; in another moment I knew he wouldn't. I knew what we had was founded on him not ever joining me and my friends, and not ever coming over and saying hi or whatever. It was all about him singling me out, pulling me out, over to him.

Of course I wasn't going to go. I wasn't going to stand up, say *Must run along now, boyfriend waiting* and go trotting off across the field.

But it made no difference really. He had my soul. He sucked it right away from me whether I wanted him to or not.

'What were you talking about?' he asked me later, on the way home from school.

'Nothing,' I said. 'I can't remember.' I hated it that he made me feel like I had to explain, apologise even. I'd done nothing wrong.

'It didn't look like nothing.' We were on the main

street, just near his road. He was walking amiably enough with his arm looped around my back but there was a metal hard note in his voice.

'Well it was nothing. Look, I can't even remember now. We were just talking.'

'I don't want you talking to those boys again.'

I laughed. I had to. What was this, the Dark Ages?

Danny's arm tightened around me. We were at the start of his road and we turned down it; he was gripping me, too hard, round the middle. 'I don't want you talking to Jacob or Miles or any of those boys,' he said.

'Don't be ridiculous!' I twisted free of his grasp. I was going to just go off home and leave him to it. No one tells me who I can and can't talk to. I turned and started walking but then he caught me by the shoulders, tight, so tight. He shook me till my head rattled. I felt such disbelief. He stopped shaking me and my eyes cleared and he was staring, right in my face, right up close, his pupils so tightened up they'd almost gone.

'No way,' I said. I shook my head and there were sparks at the sides of my eyes. 'No way.' There was a rabbit of fear scurrying up and down my spine. I pulled away, ducking his grip and started walking fast, away. Instantly he had me back. He yanked me so hard my head rocked backwards, and rocked forwards again.

'Don't you ever walk away from me,' he said into my

face, and then he shook me again. My feet were almost off the ground; I was light, floating. I could feel the numbness in my arms under his fingers where the bruises were going to be, and a rush of something *bad* fizzing up inside my head.

Suddenly he let me go; I flopped forward, limp, and he caught me again, the hands that had done me wrong holding me tenderly now. I melted into his arms like I was boneless, but that badness was buzzing behind my eyes so bright I didn't want to blink, didn't want to miss a second.

I'd never felt so alive.

He was crying now; it brought me out of myself slightly to realise it. I tried to focus my eyes but I was pressed up against the leather of his jacket; at such close distance it was black as the black inside my head. Vaguely I was aware of his hand moving around my back and stroking me. He had his face in my hair; I could hear him sobbing and I felt it against the bones of my head as he turned his face from side to side. 'Don't leave me. Don't ever leave me,' he kept on saying, over and over, till the words were burrowed in my head, stuck, forever.

Then he walked me back to his house, propping me against him as if I was an invalid. When we got there he made us tea, strong, with lots of sugar, and sat me down on the sofa in the living room, as no one else was at home. He stroked and kissed the bruises on my arms, saying, 'I love you, Louise. Don't ever leave me. Promise you'll never leave me. I couldn't live without you.'

I had this ache deep inside my chest, a tightness like my heart was being squeezed. I thought it was love.

6

Mrs Crosby was round ours again. I pushed open the back door and her voice flicked out the gap like a snake's hiss. I wished there was some way of getting an advance warning that she was there; I'd have been off round the block again, waiting till she'd gone.

Too often, Mrs Crosby was round ours.

'I was just telling your mother,' she pounced, the minute I pushed open the door, before I was even right inside, before I'd kicked off my shoes, or even had a chance to say hello, if I'd felt so inclined. 'I was just telling your mother that I saw your young man again today. When I went to the post office.'

She was sitting at the table, hands clasped tight around the obligatory cup of tea. My mother sat opposite her, fingers nervously fiddling with her teaspoon. On her face was the expression Mrs Crosby always put there, an anxious mixture of doubt and outrage. 'Hello,' I said to my mum, pointedly ignoring Mrs Crosby.

'That would be about half-past two,' Mrs Crosby went on, as though working it out to herself. Then she said a little louder, 'Shouldn't you be in school at half-past two?'

'I was,' I said, trying not to hear the disgusting sound of Mrs Crosby's tongue flicking side to side against the edges of her mouth as she planned her attack.

'I'm sure it was him,' she said, to my mother this time. 'He wears a leather jacket.'

'Lots of boys wear leather jackets,' my mum said, but I could hear the uncertainty feeding into her voice. I wanted to get a drink but I wasn't going to stay there a moment longer than I had to. At the same time, I wanted to hear whatever it was Mrs Crosby had to say. I didn't want her talking behind my back.

'Oh I don't think so,' Mrs Crosby corrected, fountain of knowledge that she was. 'My Tony never wore a leather jacket.' Her Tony was about forty now. He was big in insurance, up in Milton Keynes. *Doing ever so well*, as we frequently heard. He turned up at his mother's about twice a year in his sales rep's car, with his suit jacket hanging on a hanger against the backseat window. '*Some* boys wear leather jackets.' She nodded her head slowly, for emphasis.

'Danny's always very polite when he comes here,' my mum said uncertainly.

'I'm sure he is.' Mrs Crosby was staring at me, beady

black eyes fairly out on stalks. Here it came, the finale. 'But I do believe I saw him *smoking*.'

'You're not going to believe this,' I told Danny. We were in his room, lying stretched out side by side on his bed. He'd just lit us both a cigarette. He always lit mine when we were together; he was protective like that. 'They want to meet you properly, my mum and dad. As if they haven't already. I've got to invite you to lunch. My dad wants to give you the once over.' I blew smoke at the ceiling and waited for his response.

'That's not very nice,' he said, after an age.

'I know. It'll be awful.' I laughed, trying to make light of it. 'Really embarrassing.'

He didn't laugh back. 'I mean, it's not very nice that you don't want me to come,' he said, and his voice was cold, stilted.

'I didn't think you'd want to come,' I said. I couldn't bear it when he went all cold on me, like that.

'Why would you think that?' He was staring at the ceiling. He spoke slow and quiet but there was something else in his voice, something I couldn't understand. Little pins of fear prickled up my spine. I couldn't understand how one minute everything could be so fine, and the next it was like the sun had gone in.

Danny took a long, hard drag on his cigarette and

breathed the smoke out in three, perfect rings. 'You're ashamed of me,' he said as the third ring rose and dissipated midway to the roof.

'No I'm not!' He had to be joking. I stared at him, waiting for him to drop the hard face and laugh. He didn't.

'Then why else wouldn't you want me to come?'

'I do want you to come. Well that is, I want to see you, but not with my parents.' I sat up now, confused. I picked the ashtray up from beside the bed and stubbed out my cigarette. I wanted Danny to do the same; he was holding his cigarette upright now between his thumb and one finger, watching it burn down to the nib, ash balanced in a precarious tower. He was so controlled; I hated it, it made me nervous. I put the ashtray on his stomach. He ignored it.

'It'll just be so awful,' I tried to explain. I pushed my fingers through my hair, wishing I had my cigarette back now, just for something to do with my hands. 'They're all suspicious. Think we're up to no good. They want to get a good look at you.' Again I tried to laugh, and again he didn't. He was concentrating on that cigarette, very slowly turning it, seeing how far he could go before the ash fell. I wished he'd just stub it out and get it over with. I couldn't stand the waiting. 'You'll hate it,' I said and suddenly he blew at his hand, one short, fast breath.

Cigarette ash scattered all over us like grey snow.

'I think it's up to me to decide what I'll hate, don't you?' he said, and flicked the stunted butt into the ashtray, next to mine.

My mum was in a flap all morning. 'You might help me,' she snapped, so I cleared a space as far away from her as possible and peeled and chopped up the potatoes, and I set the table, and I loitered around, witnessing her misery. 'I've got the crumble to make yet,' she wailed all red-faced and manic, 'and the chicken's nearly done and the potatoes aren't even in. And I've still got to make the cheese sauce for your cauliflower. Why can't you eat meat like the rest of us?'

I didn't want cheese sauce. I didn't even want a cheese sandwich. I didn't want any of this and I couldn't see why she did either when it gave her so much grief. It was always like this when anyone came to lunch, which was hardly ever. She got herself wound up fit to explode, slamming things around in the kitchen and generally creating so much chaos that even though you ought to help you didn't want to go near, what with her rage hissing out at you and all those pans and knives and God knows what else piling up in the sink. Once when my aunty and uncle and my cousins came my mum stuck all the plates in the oven to warm because she said they couldn't possibly eat off cold plates; Aunty Karen *always* had warm plates when they went to her house. But she left the plates in too long so they got burning hot and then she tried to lift them out with her bare hands. She dropped them all, seven plates smashing and clattering all over the kitchen floor. The sound of it went on forever, and then there was silence. The rest of us were sat round the table in the other room, frozen.

'Oh dear,' my dad said at last with a nauseating load of resignation in his voice, and he, my aunt and I went out to the kitchen but that was the worst thing to do. As soon as she'd got an audience my mum completely lost it, getting down on her hands and knees among all those broken shards, howling like you wouldn't believe, mouth wide open, spit hanging out in strings.

She cut her hands and her knees to pieces. My dad ended up having to take her to the hospital while my aunt and I cleared up.

'Your mum's got a nervous disposition, that's the trouble,' my aunt said kindly, but I could have died of the shame.

And it was only Danny coming today, for God's sake. My boyfriend. Nothing to do with her. I couldn't believe we had to go to all this trouble just so my mum and dad could check him out, when they'd seen him plenty of times already when he called for me. Worse still, he'd really get a good look at them now. It was going to be horrendous.

Still, Danny put on a good show. He sat in the gap opposite me at the table and dolled out the charm, ladle-thick. He seemed oblivious to all the vibes flying about the table and tucked into his half-burnt chicken as if it was the best thing he'd ever eaten. My dad had the questions lined up like this was some kind of interview. How are you getting on at school? Which subject do you like best? What do you want to do when you leave?

'Music's my best subject,' Danny answered, giving it serious thought. 'I play the guitar.' This was complete rubbish. He could play the first three chords of *Smoke on the Water* but then who couldn't? 'And art. I love art.'

'Ah, Louise likes art,' my dad said, looking like he was about to suggest we all got our paints out after lunch but before he could say anything else my mum butted in.

'Yes art's all very nice but it's not a real subject, is it?' I stared at her. Of course it was a real subject. 'Not like your maths or your English. I'm always telling Louise she should concentrate more on the basics,' she said, talking about me like I wasn't there, and it was a complete lie, too. She never talked to me about what I liked at school, just whinged on about her mistakes, all the things she'd missed out on. 'On the important subjects, because they're the ones that will get her a good job. A woman needs a job she can always go back to after she's had a family. Otherwise she can end up very . . . trapped.'

'*Mum*,' I said, wishing to God she wouldn't start off down that track again. But Danny was listening to her like he was really interested and there's nothing my mum likes more than a captive audience.

'Something like teaching,' she said. 'I should have trained to be a teacher. I had the chance but, well . . . It's too late now.' She stuck her lips together, bitter-thin, and reached for the carrots, clattering the spoon against the dish. 'It's my biggest regret,' she confided to Danny in a half-whisper, just loud enough for Dad and me to hear.

I looked at my dad, wishing he'd say something, anything, to get her off the subject but he wasn't even listening. He'd switched off, the way he always did whenever she started going on.

'I like English,' Danny said. 'Especially Shakespeare. *Romeo and Juliet, Othello.*'

I almost choked on my cauliflower cheese. Where was this stuff coming from?

'I'm dead keen on drama,' he went on. 'On *theatre*. I do love the theatre.'

He was looking at me as he spoke. I searched his face for some kind of indication that he was taking the piss but found none. I do believe he meant what he said. And he was right about loving the theatre. Boy, could he act.

After lunch we went for a walk, Danny and me.

'God that was awful,' I said, as soon as we were out of the house.

He didn't say anything. He just walked along beside me, hand looped around my waist. He was staring into the middle distance with a frown on his face, distracted. God knows what he thought about my parents, and me, now.

We walked down to the watersplash, at the end of his road, and stopped on the bridge. When we got there he lit a cigarette and handed it to me. Then he lit one for himself, and leaned forward over the railings, staring down at the water. I watched him take a deep drag on his cigarette, then as he let the smoke out his mouth he inhaled it straight back in again, back up his nose. He hadn't said a word since we'd left my house.

'Sorry,' I said, at last, when I couldn't stand the silence any more.

He took another drag, then kind of slumped down on his elbows. He seemed really *sad.*

'My mum's just so embarrassing. And my dad drives me nuts the way he just sits there, letting her say all that stuff. And I didn't know he was going to interrogate you. *What do you want to do when you leave school?* Honestly—'

'At least you've got a dad,' Danny muttered, cutting me off.

I stared at him. I didn't know what to say.

He flicked his cigarette into the water. 'At least you've got a dad,' he repeated and the catch in his voice ripped at my heart. 'At least your dad isn't *dead*.'

'Oh God I'm so sorry.' I put my hand on his shoulder and he turned to me and I held him in my arms. He was crying, really crying. I could feel him shaking and he held on to me so tight. His pain sliced through me and I was crying too. I'd had no idea. I mean, I knew his dad wasn't around but I'd just presumed his parents were divorced or something. I didn't know his dad was *dead*.

'He died when I was ten,' he sobbed into my hair. 'Died in his sleep. Mum woke up one morning and he was dead beside her. Gone.'

My poor, poor Danny. It explained so much. So much of the weirdness. We stood there for ages, just clinging to each other. Stood there while some old guy shuffled past us with his dog sniffing at our ankles.

Vaguely I heard the man moaning about us blocking the path and did our parents know what we were up to, but I didn't care. I didn't care about anything except Danny. He needed me. And I'd have forgiven him anything then, anything.

Yet not so long after this I called round at Danny's house on a Sunday afternoon, and his dad was there. In the living room, deep in discussion with his mum, and very much alive. He called us into the room, just as we were about to go out. Wanted to get a look at me, he said, and he sat on the sofa, giving me the once over and cracking jokes. I tried to smile but I couldn't, not with Danny scowling away beside me and his mother doing her best to hide the fact that she was sitting there crying, and this man, supposed to be dead.

'Done all right for yourself there, son,' he barked, loud-voiced and wheezy, slapping his hands down on his oversized thighs. Danny said nothing; I could feel the tension in him, electric.

Maybe it's his stepfather, I thought. But if you took away the bald head and a layer of fat and knocked off however many years it could be Danny sitting there, same blue eyes, same turned-up nose.

'Tosser,' Danny muttered, as soon as we were outside.

'Who?' I asked.

'My dad,' he said, like he'd completely forgotten he'd ever told me he was dead.

Carefully, I said, 'I didn't think your dad was around any more.'

'He isn't normally,' Danny said, 'and I wish he'd hurry up and go away again.'

I don't think Danny *lied* as such. I think he really believed the things he said, when he said them. I believed him too, most of the time. But it was like he had this whole other reality going on, inside his head.

7

The concert was on the last day of term. Right up until the last minute I thought I was going with Cara. She'd put herself out to tolerate the fact that I was seeing Danny, especially as it freed Jacob up for her.

We were going to meet at Cara's an hour beforehand, Emma and me, to get ready.

Danny wasn't even going. Every time I'd mentioned it Danny had said, 'Do me a favour, end of term concerts? I think I grew out of that at Juniors,' or 'Why would I want to go and see some plastic never-has-been never-will-be screeching to a bunch of hysterical girls?'

I didn't mind, though. I was glad to be going with Cara and Emma. It would kind of spoil things or at the very least make things awkward if one of us turned up with a boyfriend in tow. I knew Cara wanted to get off with Jacob, which probably wouldn't happen. But what mattered was that we'd go together, start off together.

But on the morning of the concert Danny was waiting for me on the corner of his road. I knew he'd got there early and been there a while because he was agitated, kicking at a loose stone on the pavement with his foot, and drawing on his cigarette through the fingers of his cupped fist, watching for me.

'I'm going with you tonight,' he said, straight away.

'You haven't got a ticket.' I know I should have been pleased, but the words were out before I could stop them. I saw the hardness set in his eyes before he turned, and started walking. I trotted along beside him, trying to make what I'd just said sound better. 'I mean I really want you to come, you know I do, but how will you get in without a ticket?'

'I'll get in,' he said, without looking at me. 'I don't need a ticket.'

Danny had this thing, this other-worldliness about him, a kind of *godliness*. It wasn't arrogance, or conceit. Not really. He genuinely believed that tickets and timetables and rules and all those other conformities that map out all our lives simply didn't apply to him. I suppose it was this self-belief that made him so special, but I still didn't think he'd get into the Leila Mars concert without a ticket. How could he? There'd been enough letters sent home about security to keep the paper-recycling in business for months.

Not that I'd point this out, of course.

What I did say, equally stupidly, was, 'I was going with Cara.'

Danny stopped walking, but he didn't look at me. He

took a short, angry drag on his cigarette and threw it down hard onto the pavement. He stood still then, eyes shut for a second, like there was a pain passing through him. And then he walked on. I shadowed his moves. I walked, I stopped, I walked again. I hung in the air, I followed.

'We planned it ages ago,' I said, trying to explain. 'You didn't want to come.'

'You don't want me to come,' Danny said.

'Of course I do—'

'Cara doesn't want me to come,' he said now, so swiftly turning things around. And he stopped, and he looked at me, and he smiled a sad, half-smile, shaking his head at the same time. 'I can't understand you,' he said. 'You say you love me but when it comes down to it—'

'I do love you,' I cut in but it just fired him up more.

'How can I believe you when you act like this?' he asked, all incredulous now. 'When you'd rather be with Cara than with me? Cara, who'd like nothing better than to break us up?'

I was going to speak, to say *that isn't true* but he beat me to it, saying, 'You know she's trying to split us up, don't you? You know that's what she wants?'

And I hesitated for a second, because he had a point. Cara didn't like him, she never had.

Danny put his hands on my arms, and started stroking them up and down. 'Why are you doing this to me, Louise?' he said and he was pleading with me now. '*Why?*' The pain in his voice got hold of my heart and twisted it. 'I love you so much, Louise,' he said and when he spoke to me like that everything else, *everything*, just faded away. 'How can you let anyone come between us?'

I stared into his eyes, so, so blue.

'Who do you care about most?' he asked, and it was a real question, he really meant it. 'Cara or me?'

I told Cara after registration. I wanted to just get it over with.

'Danny's coming tonight,' I said, trying to sound like that was a good thing.

Cara said nothing but she let her face slip as she looked at me, except for her eyebrows, which remained cynically high.

'He wants me to go with him.'

Cara picked up her bag and started walking out the room. She didn't say a word.

'Well he *is* my boyfriend,' I called after her, trying to justify things, to myself if not to her. 'And I'll still see you there.'

But she was already gone, down the corridor.

* * *

'Cara's really upset,' I said to Danny at lunchtime. We were lying on the grass up by the houses at the back of the school. It was a really hot day, humid, and with no air, like the sky was pressing down. I lay flat on my back, with my arm up across my forehead to shield my eyes. Every time I turned my head I could feel the start of a headache, throbbing up.

'Well she would be,' Danny said. He was leaning up on his elbow, and with his other hand he was stroking the skin on my chest, trailing a pattern up and across my collar bone and down into the opening of my shirt. He stroked his fingers rhythmically, following the movement of his hand with his eyes.

I turned to look at him, and pain shot across the back of my eyes. 'I feel really bad,' I said. 'We were all going to get ready together, at her house. We'd been planning it for ages.'

I don't know what I expected. Maybe for him to say, *Well OK you go with Cara, and I'll see you there.*

Would that have been too much to ask for?

I don't think so. But then if it mattered that much to me why didn't I just do what I wanted and go with Cara anyway?

I don't know. Too many things I don't know.

Danny's hand stilled. In the heat it felt heavy, lying

there, right over my heart. White, killing sunlight was hitting right into the corner of my eye but I squinted through it. Danny's eyes moved from the pattern he'd drawn on my chest, and up to my face. He had his own shade, looking down. I had all the brightness; I had to stare right into it, just to see him. I stared so hard I could see double.

'She'll get over it,' Danny said, and maybe I should have been annoyed. Maybe I would have been if the heat and the ache in my head weren't numbing me out so. He laughed a short, harsh laugh. It cracked in my ears. 'Sometimes you're so naïve I can't believe it,' he said. 'She's jealous. You've got to know that. She's jealous because you've got a boyfriend and she hasn't.'

He bent down over me, and his weight came down through his hand and into my chest. For a moment I couldn't breathe. But then he kissed me and I didn't want to breathe, I didn't want to think, I wanted just to blot out the pain inside my head.

I let my parents carry on thinking I was still going round to Cara's before the concert, just so I could go out early, and not have to sit through another terminal family mealtime.

I couldn't wait to get out of the house.

My mum had been in a mood for days, because of the way my dad had chopped back the camellia bush in the front garden.

'Look at it! Just look at it! You've done it all wrong,' she'd wailed at him, scabby red hands clawing at her temples like it was all just too much.

And to try and make a better job of it my dad had gone back out with his shears and hacked off some more, as if he was dumb enough to think that would please her. Nothing would please her. Nothing, ever, ever, ever. Surely he knew that by now.

'Ruined! Ruined!' she kept wailing, like anyone cared. I just wanted to get the sound of her voice right out of my head.

It was a fucking plant, for God's sake. It would grow back.

They had a big fight once. Years ago, when I was about seven. I say it was a big fight but what I really mean is my dad lost it with her endless moaning on. She'd flung a cup of tea at him, from across the kitchen. I remember sitting at the other side of the table from my dad and watching tea run orange down his face, and orange down the wall. Whole seconds went by and he sat there, and the look on his face had me pinned rigid in my chair, more terrified than I'd ever be by my mum's ranting on. Even she was frightened; I could tell because she'd stopped yelling at him at last and stood still, waiting for what came next. We were all waiting.

He didn't wipe his face. He put both his hands on the table, pushed back his chair and stood up. And he walked slowly over to her, march, march, march. I thought he was going to hit her. She thought it too; I saw her flinch in anticipation. My heart picked up speed. *Go on*, I was thinking, *do it, do it*.

But he didn't.

He loomed right over her, pointing his finger into her face.

'Don't – you – ever – do – that – again,' he said, punctuating each word with a pause and a jab of that finger. Then he picked up his car keys from the side, went out the back door and we didn't see him again for two days.

I don't know where he went. No one's ever thought it necessary to tell me. I just remember crying and crying because my dad had gone and I thought he was dead. And my mum not getting out of her dressing-gown for the whole two days and saying nothing, *nothing*, to make me feel any better.

And then he came back, but instead of being happy again I felt angry. Angry that he'd gone in the first place and angry that he was back, and didn't seem to consider the ordeal he'd put me through. And when I saw him pussy-footing around her again I felt angrier still.

And here he was now, taking all that crap over a fucking bush.

When I was little I used to lie in my bed at night and think myself out of my body. I'd kind of float myself up into another place, and look down. I'd see little me sleeping in my pink spotty pyjamas, and I'd look around my room, at all my toys and things. It all looked so alien.

I was convinced I was adopted, and I used to imagine where my real family were, and what they were like. Lots of kids do this, I suppose, just to put a bit of romance in to their existence. But I really meant it. I just couldn't believe that I had come from *them*.

They were still arguing when I went out. The gut-churning echo of their misery rolled around the house, my mum's voice, high-pitched and grating, firing off like a sniper gun; *You never do this, you never do that, why do you always* . . . God it went on and on. I wanted to stick my fist in her mouth. I wanted to just shut her up. And my dad's deep voice worn so far down it was just a mumble, droning away, placating her all the time.

I don't know who I hated most, her for going on all the time or him for just taking it.

'I'm going out now!' I yelled from the hallway, in case anyone was interested.

My mum stopped nagging my dad for a second to poke her head out from the kitchen. 'You haven't eaten yet!' she snapped.

'I'll get something at Cara's,' I said. I could barely look at her with her eyes all red and her hair sticking up like she'd been clawing at it.

'How will you get home?'

'I'll walk back with Danny. He's going too.' I opened the front door. I just wanted to get out of there, before she started on me now.

'Well don't be late—'

I closed the door behind me, cutting her off. And it was just such a relief, to be out of that house, though I still had the pitch of her voice ringing in my ears, halfway up the road.

No one had thought to wish me a nice time or anything. But then why would they? Having a nice time wasn't something you did, in our house.

Danny's mum let me in. She opened the front door and Charlie, their cat, shot out past my legs.

'Charlie!' she shouted after it, pulling me in and half closing the door, too late now the cat had gone. 'Hello, love,' she said to me, wiping her hands on a tea towel.

'That stupid cat. He keeps wandering off and getting lost.' She opened the front door again then hesitated; something on the cooker was getting close to a burn. 'Oh, the bacon,' she said and dashed back to the kitchen. I followed her, and loitered in the doorway as she snatched the frying pan off the hob. Sparks of fat sizzled up, dancing across her hand and she caught her breath on a hiss and put the pan back down, flicked that tea towel around the handle, and picked it up again to slide the bacon out onto plates already piled up with chips. Then she stuck the pan in the sink, turned on the tap and the sizzling turned to a roar. The air was so thick I could taste it.

'Ellie!' Danny's mum yelled over her shoulder. 'Ellie, go and call Charlie back in. I'm in the middle of dishing up tea.'

Danny's little sister slunk out of the living room. 'You look nice,' she said to me, slyly, putting her fat little hand out to touch my skirt. She'd got purple glitter painted on the stubs of her nails. 'Are you going to a party?'

'We're going to a concert,' I said.

'Oh, Louise,' Danny's mum said, like she'd just remembered I was there. 'Here, take this up to Danny. He's in his room. Save me calling him down.' She shoved a plate at me and a couple of chips fell off, onto the floor. 'Oh never mind them, Charlie'll have them,' she said and she wiped her hand across her forehead, pink from the heat of cooking. 'Ellie, will you go out and call him. *Go on.*'

Ellie didn't want to go. Ellie was too busy pawing at my clothes. 'Do you love my brother?' she weedled. 'Are you going to snog him?'

Danny's sister could be sweet in small doses but most of the time I agreed with Danny; she was a total pain in the backside.

I went upstairs and banged on Danny's door but he didn't answer so I turned the handle with my free hand and bumped it open with my hip, trying not to tip up the plate.

He was lying on his bed, naked apart from his jeans, listening to a CD. Seeing me, he took off his headphones and the music rattled out, distorted.

'Waitress service,' I said, and sat down on the bed beside him, with the plate balanced on my knees.

'You're early,' he said.

'I couldn't wait to get out. My parents were driving me nuts, fighting over some stupid bush in the garden.'

He sat up, leaning against me while we ate. I could feel the skin of his chest against my bare arm, hot.

'You're stealing all my chips,' he said.

'I'm starving.'

'You don't really want to go to this concert, do you?' He took the plate off my knees, and put it on the floor, and lay back down, taking me with him.

'I do,' I said, but my heart was speeding up. He'd got his arms around me, tight and he pulled me over so I was lying on top of him, stretched out.

'You know it'll be total crap.' Then he was kissing me and I knew where this was going; his hands were working their way down my back and inside my clothes, drawing shivers across my skin. I wriggled against him and he groaned.

'We can't,' I said.

'We can,' he mumbled into my neck.

'Your mum's downstairs.'

'She never comes up.' He pushed me up so I was sitting on him. I'd got my short black skirt on; it would be so easy to do it, just like that. He was thinking it; I was thinking it. Seconds later we *were* doing it then suddenly we heard the door click and the scrape of it dragging against the carpet, just a fraction. We both froze, staring at each other. I couldn't even breathe. Then we heard a giggle and Danny pushed me off, sideways.

'Fuck off, Ellie,' he yelled and lightning quick he grabbed up the ashtray from beside the bed and hurled it. It hit the door but even so Ellie squealed like a pig and ran screaming downstairs.

'Shit!' Danny hissed.

In the seconds it took us to get our clothes back together Danny's mum was at the bottom of the stairs, calling, 'Danny! Danny! You get down here!'

'I'll fucking kill her,' Danny muttered, sticking his feet into his trainers and pulling on a T-shirt at the same time. He flung open the door and ran out onto the landing. Slowly I followed, thinking that I'd die if Ellie had actually seen anything. And God – what if she told her mum?

'What have you done to Ellie?' Danny's mum demanded. She was standing on the stairs now, blocking the way. Ellie was just behind her, wailing her head off.

'Move,' Danny barked. 'I'm going to kill the little bitch,' and he tried to get past his mum but she had one hand on the banister and one hand on the wall, stopping him.

'Oh no you won't,' she said, and that wailing behind her got louder. 'What have you done to her?'

'She was snooping at my door,' Danny shouted. 'Spying on us.'

'He threw something at me,' Ellie howled and carried on with her bawling.

'What do you think you're doing, throwing things at her? She's half your size—'

'*Don't* fucking start.' Danny's voice was like ice. From

behind him I saw the colour rise in his mum's face, I saw fear flicker in her eyes.

'Danny,' I said but he took no notice. He stuck his face up so close to his mum's that she had to lean back. He grabbed hold of her arm where she was holding the banister, and pushed her back against the wall, hard. Ellie screamed and ran into the kitchen, banging the door shut behind her.

'Danny!' I said again and I ran down the stairs and took hold of his arm. For a second I thought he was going to shove me away too. I could feel the tension under his skin, rigid.

'Oh why don't you all just fuck off!' he shouted and he kicked the little table in the hall so all the papers stacked up on it flew off and scattered out across the floor. Then he slammed his way out of the front door, taking me with him.

We walked for miles. Across the watersplash at the end of his road, and down onto the main road and left, all the way past the council depot. There's nothing out that way, except a row of old houses that no one's lived in for years, and an ancient petrol station that had closed up ages ago. Most of the fields up that end have been bought up by developers but nothing's been built yet; a few of the trees have been flattened and the ground dug up, and white, wooden fences slapped up along the edge of the road, but nothing else. A couple of bulldozers sat where they'd sat for weeks, slowly sinking into the mud.

We walked fast; *Danny* walked fast with all that anger driving him. He walked like he couldn't get away from it. He didn't speak, I didn't speak. I don't think he even knew where he was going. He just walked and walked, with his hand locked tight onto mine, pulling me along beside him.

There was an alleyway up the side of the old petrol station. Once, you could have got a car up there but now it was almost completely clogged with nettles grown waist-high and brambles so dense that they'd knotted together, blocking the path. Danny picked up a stick and started hacking us a way through. It seemed mad to me to even try, but Danny was determined; he hacked at those bushes like he really meant it, like he was beating out his anger.

I clung on to his hand. I'd got nettle stings all over my legs and my heart was hammering with the effort of not getting myself ripped to shreds by thorns. Then suddenly we were through, and standing on a large slab of concrete out the back of the petrol station, hemmed in on three sides by a wall. This would be where they'd kept the bins, or done things to cars; there were oil stains all over the concrete. Someone else had been here before us, recently, though I wondered how they'd got there. There were fag butts on the ground and a couple of squashed-up beer cans, and the faint smell of piss, coming from the corners.

We sat down, on a cleanish bit of ground. I sat on the edge of my skirt, with my knees drawn up, and pressed my fingers down on the nettle stings on my legs to try and stop the tingling. Still Danny hadn't said anything. But he wanted me there, I know he did. Look how tight he'd held my hand.

He picked up a broken chunk of concrete by his leg and threw it at a beer can, over by the wall. He missed, and it landed by what looked like a dried-up lump of something. Dog shit? Who knows? It was a desolate place to be pissed off in.

At last he spoke. 'This place fucks me up,' he said. 'All of it. Fucking people, fucking on my case all the time.' He dug his hand into his back pocket and fished out his cigarette packet, squashed so flat he had to stick his fingers in to prise it open. He tipped it up on the ground in front of him. Out fell three bent cigarettes and a miniscule scrap of dope, wrapped up in cling film. It was so small you had to be desperate to bother, but Danny was desperate. He ripped open a couple of cigarettes and we got one, skinny joint out of it. 'One day,' he said, when he'd got it burning, 'I am going to get so out of here.'

'Me too.'

He passed the joint to me, careful that it didn't fall apart. 'We'll go away, together, you and me.' He struck out his arm, cutting through the air. 'Soon. We'll go away soon.'

It was rubbish dope. The sort that gives you a headache, and nothing else. I could feel it fogging me up.

'Except you don't want to be with me.'

I stared at him. 'What do you mean?'

'You'd rather be with Jacob fucking Warren than with me.'

'No, I wouldn't.' I couldn't believe he was saying this. It was the dope talking, it had to be.

He took back the joint and laughed a short, harsh laugh. 'Yes you would. You'd rather be at that stupid concert with him.'

'For God's sake, Danny.'

'Look at you in your short skirt. Do you want every bloke in Eppingham looking at you?'

'Of course I don't.' Even so I tried to pull my skirt down a little, over my thighs.

He drew hard on that spliff and it flared up, right up to his fingers. 'You could have any bloke and you know it,' he said. 'What would you want to be with me for?'

'Because I love you . . .'

'How do I know that you won't fuck me up like everyone else?'

'Because I won't.' I was crying now. It was always like this. He'd suddenly turn, and go on and on saying these things till he'd got me crying.

'But how do I *know* that?' The way he was looking at me no answer would ever be enough. He crumbled the smouldering remains of that joint between his fingers. 'How?' he said again, and I could hear the pain in his voice, so real.

'Because it's true. I don't want to be with anyone else. But you drive me away when you talk like this.' I put my head on my knees. I wished I hadn't smoked that dope; it just made things worse. Danny put his arm around me; he put his head against mine.

'You're all I've got,' he said, stroking his hand across my hair. 'I couldn't bear to lose you.'

'Then don't,' I whispered and he was kissing me now, kissing my face, my neck, and down inside my shirt where he'd got it undone.

'I don't know what I'd do without you,' he said, and he pushed me back, down onto the concrete. I could feel my hair sticking to the oil. 'I love you so much. I *need* you.' He was on top of me now, and undoing his jeans. 'Don't ever leave me,' he said. 'Promise me. Promise you'll never leave me.'

'I promise,' I said and I meant it. I swear I did. I meant it.

So I never did get to the concert. But Danny was probably right anyway. It would have just been a load of plastic pop and a load of plastic girls, screaming.

8

I knew Cara would be pissed off with me, so I called her, first thing, to get it over with.

And I laid it on dead thick, about Danny having this big fight with his mum, and being so upset and everything. Though of course I didn't tell her what had started it.

'It was awful,' I told her. 'And I can't believe I ended up missing the concert.'

'Can't you?' Cara said, all sarcastic, and I felt the heat buzz up into my ears. What right did she have to be so judgmental?

'I didn't plan to miss it,' I said. 'But what could I do? Danny was really upset. I couldn't just leave him, could I?'

She didn't say anything, she didn't need to; the silence said it all. And to think I'd actually expected some sympathy, once I'd told her what had happened.

'You know that I really wanted to go,' I said but I could tell she didn't believe me. She'd be in a sulk for days now, and I didn't feel much like grovelling. 'Well anyway, what was it like?' I asked, somewhat half-heartedly.

'Actually,' Cara said, 'it was fantastic.'

Danny had said all along that Cara wanted to split us up. Now I could see he was right.

She just couldn't accept him. She couldn't see past his image, past his *reputation*, for want of a better word. And it was like she expected me to make a choice somehow, him or her.

But to me there was no choice. She should have known that.

I didn't call Cara again. There didn't seem much point.

So in the holidays I just went around with Danny all the time, and sometimes we saw his friends, Richard and this guy Mikey Petes, who lived up Danny's road and was in the year below us at school. Mikey was off his head most of the time and even when he wasn't he couldn't keep still, not for a second, he was just so wired. He had this weird laugh that came out of him in a burst, high-pitched and staccato, like he'd been breathing in helium. And he always had some dope on him. He got it off his mate Bez. I never met Bez, though I heard enough about him. Enough to know he was older than all of us and that Danny, Richard and Mikey seemed to think he was some kind of demi-god, though I thought he sounded more like a total nutter.

My mum had it in her head that Danny and I were

dating now, though we never really went anywhere. If we were lucky Danny's mum would go out and we'd get to babysit and have the house to ourselves. Other times if he had any money Danny'd buy a bottle of vodka from the off licence down by the station. The guy in there'd sell anything to anyone.

'How old are you?' he'd ask every time, looking us up and down.

'Eighteen,' Danny would always reply, and it was obvious the man didn't believe him but he didn't bother asking us for ID, just sold us the stuff anyway. Danny reckoned he was a sad old perv and we were doing him a favour, just going into the shop, and it was true, the guy did have a bit of a leer on him.

Then we'd take the vodka to the boathouse and drink it, and make all these plans. Plans about running away, where we'd go, what we'd need. It all seemed so possible when there was just us, and the vodka, and maybe a little bit of dope. In my head I'd got my bag packed; I'd got this mental list of what I'd need, the essentials; my mascara, my cleanser, my black jumper that goes with everything. I'd lie there in Danny's arms, ticking it off in my head while he talked all these dreams, all these way-up, glorious dreams.

One night I remember Danny'd walked me back home and we were outside my house, kissing. I remember how I felt – drunk and stoned and so high on Danny that my head was spinning right out of itself. I was holding on to him, half falling backwards and we were kissing and laughing at the same time and that poisonous witch Mrs Crosby came scuttling out from next door to see what was going on. She was watching us from behind her bushes, trying to get a good look. We could see her purple slippers, sticking out from under the hedge.

'Good evening, there,' Danny said and the bush shivered and the slippers disappeared, and I thought I'd kill myself, laughing.

Sometimes, like if it was raining and we had nowhere else to go, we'd go and see this guy Doug who Danny knew, from the year above us. Doug was a bit of a weirdo, into war memorabilia and stuff like that; he didn't have many friends. I don't know how Danny knew him, and it was as if he was doing Doug a favour, just by hanging around with him from time to time.

Doug's house was right up the other end of Eppingham, twenty minutes' walk away. Danny'd buy some beer or vodka if he could afford it and we'd just turn up, and Doug would always be in. His mum or dad or brother would answer the door; *he's upstairs*, they'd say and we'd go on up, up the steep stairs that led into the attic of their bungalow, where his bedroom was.

Danny would tap on the door and we'd go straight in; it never occurred to us that Doug might be busy, that he might not want to see us. His room was big and very tidy with shelves against one wall and his bed opposite and a great unfilled space in between. Over his bed he had a huge poster of a topless woman in a thong, all glossy lips and dewy brown eyes. Danny said it didn't matter that we never told Doug we'd be coming; he'd only be up in his room tossing himself off anyway.

Recently, I heard that Doug quit the sixth form and went off and joined a police training college instead. I can't imagine him as a policeman. But then I can't imagine why he let us keep coming round, unless Danny was right and he was desperate for friends. He let us in, and never drank any of our vodka or whatever so we drank it ourselves, sitting on his bed. There was one chair in the room. Doug sat on that and just sort of watched us. We never really talked to him much, we just drank the drink and got on with the snogging, lying back on the bed while Doug just sat there looking at us. We never actually went all the way, not quite, but after half a bottle of vodka or whatever the numbness softened things so that Doug's presence seemed cosy; he seemed one of us and I just got so used to it and so drunk that I easily could have gone all the way. Only Danny liked to make this big show about being all protective. We'd lie there and things would go just so far then he'd pull my clothes together again, covering me up, as if that showed that he cared.

Once, Doug had a party. Well, that is, Danny had a party, at Doug's house.

Doug's parents were away so Danny went round telling everyone to be round his house, that night. Only about ten people came in the end but at least Bez didn't turn up, though Danny spent most of the night saying he would. Doug let us all in and we sat around in his parents' living room with its crystal ornaments and immaculate three piece suite, while Danny acted like it was his house, going out to the kitchen to find biscuits and sorting through the dodgy CD collection for some half-decent music. And we sat around, smoking and drinking, and trying not to laugh at Doug's face getting more and more anxious by the second.

Then Danny coughed, all theatrical, to get everyone's attention, and pulled me to him, and said, 'Excuse me but I've a little something to attend to.' And he led me from the room, upstairs to Doug's room just like he owned the place and then we did do it, on Doug's bed, and he loved them all knowing we were doing it. Afterwards, we went straight back downstairs, and with them all watching he lit two cigarettes, one for me, one for him, just in case they were in any doubt. No one smirked, no one dared to, but they all knew and a couple of the guys moved up to make room for me on the sofa and Danny fetched me a drink, said, 'There you are, darling,' and if I tried to tell you now how that made me feel all I could say is that I felt the way Danny wanted me to feel: *claimed.*

Danny carried a Durex in his wallet, always, just in case. His friends all knew it was there; he liked that. Whenever he got his wallet out, and he did, often, he'd let the Durex fall out, tuck it back in, say, 'Oops, don't want to lose that' or 'Might be needing that later.' He wanted everyone to know and I went along with this. It seemed OK because he loved me, I knew he did. I always knew it, I never doubted it, not then, not now, not for a moment.

At the beginning of August I had to go to France for two weeks with my mum and dad. We went every year, to the same place, a campsite near La Rochelle, where some guy my dad knew had a caravan. In the weeks before we went my mum would wash and iron and fold up clothes into piles till you ended up with nothing to wear; she was manic, she even ironed and folded up knickers and stuck them in the case, two weeks in advance. I mean for God's sake; everything was always creased up when we got there anyway and who cared? Except my mum, who spent the first two or three days we were there crying over the state of things as she shook them out – *look at the creases, look at them, just look at them* – and then crying some more over the fact that there wasn't enough space to hang everything. Though you'd think she'd know that by now, as we'd been going there every year, for the last forever at least.

I didn't want to go. I never wanted to go, but this year I really didn't. I didn't want to be away from Danny.

Two weeks hung before us like a very long time.

'Stay,' Danny said, and he held me so tight, like I was leaving him forever. 'Stay here with me.'

But how could I?

The night before I went, we went to the boathouse. He'd brought a candle, that he lit, and balanced on the floor.

'Take off your clothes,' he said. His face was eerie in the flickering light. 'I want to look at you. At all of you.'

So I took off my clothes and stood there as he covered every centimetre of my body with his eyes; my front, my back, my sides. In the chill of the air I could feel goosebumps breaking out on my skin as he lifted my arms, and turned my hands to study my palms and my fingers. He crouched down and pushed my feet apart so he could see the insides of my legs; then he lifted my feet one by one, and looked at the soles underneath and at the gaps in between my toes. He held my hand to balance me, then he kissed it, and let it go. Then he stood up again and scooped my hair away from the back of my neck, then lowered it again, so gently, and stroked it back behind my ears, right back, so he could see the skin there, along the edge of my hairline. I felt his breath on my neck; the goosebumps shifted, shrank, then rose up again.

Trance-like I stood there and let him do all this. He made me feel so wanted. More than wanted. He made me feel *owned*.

'I'll know if anyone else touches you, Louise,' he whispered, trailing his fingertip gently along my jawline, from my ear to my chin. His voice prickled my ear.

I wanted to laugh at the very idea. 'They won't,' I said but it came out more like a croak.

Slowly he walked around me, till we were face to face again. His eyes were so, so dark, night-black, like the sky. 'I'll know,' he said again. 'I've got you in here.'

And he tapped the side of his head with his finger, hard, tap, tap tap.

I texted him loads of times, every day. He wanted me to phone him too, every night at seven o'clock. My phone didn't work from France so I had to go down to the campsite call box, and stuff my money into the pay-slot, with my heart clogging up, anxious, nervous, and just plain desperate to hear his voice.

I did miss him. In France the night sky was so much clearer than at home, and you could see all these stars, so many of them, bright against the inky black. I'd wander down to the kids' playground after I'd phoned him and sit on one of the swings and stare up at the sky, thinking it was the same sky over Danny's head, and if he couldn't see the stars so well at home at least he'd see the moon the same, if he looked up. The moon would be the same the world over, the same half-circle, clouding out at the side.

Of course, now I know that isn't true. Now I know you get a different view of the moon, wherever you are. You wouldn't even see it at all if it was hidden behind clouds. But still, the illusion was nice, at the time. It was what I wanted to think, and my whole life was altered by what I wanted to think, back then.

On our last night we went into La Rochelle for dinner. We went at about six and didn't get back until late, and I didn't get the chance to phone Danny. I texted him, though, in the car. I told him why I couldn't phone. *I'll see you tomorrow*, I wrote. *Can't wait.*

I didn't think it was a problem. Really I didn't. I had no idea, not until I went round to see him, the minute we got back.

I'd bought him a knife. The sort of thing you'd never get here but there was this shop in one of the villages we went to in France that had them all over the walls. Some of them were so huge you could chop someone's head off; they were incredible, you'd think they couldn't possibly be real. The one I got Danny was small, about twelve centimetres long and slim, with a black handle.

My parents didn't know I'd got it, of course. They'd have gone mad. I smuggled it in among my clothes and things and I didn't give it another thought, except that Danny would love it.

He peeled off the tissue paper now, and stared down at the knife, turning it in his hand. 'Thanks,' he said, and that was it. I'd been so looking forward to seeing him. I'd imagined his face when he saw me again, I'd imagined throwing myself into his arms. But there'd been none of that. Just this strange . . . distance. His mum had opened the door to me and sent me on up to his room. He didn't kiss me when he saw me. He didn't even smile.

I sat beside him on his bed and there was a cold worm snaking its warning path up my spine. 'Do you like it?' I asked but what I really meant was, do you still like me?

He turned the knife over in his hand one more time then held it still, as if feeling its weight. 'It's great,' he said at last, but with such leaden finality in his voice. I could feel my heartbeat, picking up speed. It was like he didn't even want to look at me.

'What's wrong?' I whispered.

'You didn't phone on Friday,' he said and my heart stopped a second before it burst out again, pounding.

Half of me wanted to laugh, out of relief. God, if that was all this was about then it was nothing; I didn't phone on Friday because I was stuck with my parents, witnessing their pathetic annual attempt at finding some kind of joy in their joyless existence. I'd told him that when I'd texted him; I could tell him it again, now.

Only with Danny things were never so straight forward.

'I told you to phone me.' He looked at me now, but you could never read anything in those eyes. Stupidly, seeing as I'd bought it, I wished he'd put the knife down.

'I couldn't,' I said. 'I had to go out, with my parents.' He carried on looking at me, face dead still. He made me so nervous; like I was *guilty*. 'I told you.'

'But how can I believe you?' he asked and there was that pleading note in his voice now, the one that undid me every time. 'You could have phoned if you wanted to. You could have found a phone.'

It flashed through my head and he saw it: I'm in that

restaurant, looking around; there's the bar at the back and beyond that the stairs down to the loo. Was there a phone? Was there?

'You could have phoned,' he said again. 'But you didn't want to.'

'I did want to.'

He stared at me, saying nothing.

'I was out with my parents.' I had to whisper; I could feel my voice fading out.

'You keep saying that. But how do I know it's true?'

'Because it *is* true! Of course it's true.' Now it was me doing the pleading but how pathetic I sounded. How *feeble*. I should have phoned. I should have found a way. It was written all over his face and he was right: I could have found a way. 'I'm sorry,' I whispered.

Danny looked down and that was worse; he was shutting me out.

'I'm sorry,' I said again. I didn't know what else I could say. I didn't know what I should do. Was that it? *Over?*

'I don't know what you do when you're away from me,' Danny muttered, still staring down at that knife in his hands. 'I don't know who you're with.'

I was shaking now, and crying. I couldn't think of anything else to say, just 'I'm sorry,' over and over.

'It eats me up,' he said and suddenly he jolted his legs

out straight and his hands followed, like in a kind of spasm, and the knife fell down onto the floor between his feet. 'It kills me –' he pushed his hands into his hair, clutching at his head '– thinking what you might be doing. Thinking of some other bloke, touching you.'

'No, Danny, never,' I said. 'Never, I promise.'

'I couldn't stand it,' he said and he looked at me again, so intent. I pulled back; I had to, just to take in the strength of that stare. 'I could – not – stand – it.' And then he was all wistful suddenly, gentle, drawing me back. 'I love you,' he said, so tenderly, and I tried to say it back but I was crying too much. 'You're everything to me, everything.'

He wanted to see me naked again. To see if I had changed, but of course I hadn't. Of course I was still his, always would be. He peeled off my clothes and made me lie back on his bed. Then, still fully clothed himself he looked me over, from the top of my head to the soles of my feet. And when he'd finished with the front of me, he turned me over, and started on the back, and then on the sides. He took his time, like he did in the boathouse, as if he thought he might find a lie somewhere. And only when he'd searched every part of me could he give himself up at last, and take off his own clothes, and lose himself in me, again.

I could stop here. I could blink my eyes and say that

was it; we had the summer, the long, glorious summer. I could parcel it up, and stop here.

We had all these plans, for forever. Everyone does, I suppose.

We said we'd have a daughter one day. She'd have the bluest eyes you ever saw, and hair like mine, black and wild. We even had a name for her: Aqua-Marie. Sometimes we played with the fates and took a gamble at making her.

It never happened, and I suppose I should be grateful for that.

But we had all these plans. Neither of us could see an end, not ever.

He had this calendar, hung from a nail banged into his wall, above his CD player. It was one of those big, wall chart calendars with no pictures or anything, just the years' months in little boxes all on one sheet; the sort that you'd get free at a petrol station or in a magazine around Christmas or whatever. On it he'd drawn a line through the second week of each month because that was when he thought my period was due. It probably was once, when he began all this, but I was never that regular. He'd even marked it out on the small sections on the top and bottom of the calendar, showing last year and next year. It didn't matter that it wasn't accurate. What mattered was that it was marked out for everyone to see, for him to see. It meant that he knew about me, that we were permanent.

He even referred to his bedroom as our room. Sometimes his mates came round while I was there; Richard, and Mikey. Danny's mum would answer the door and call up to him. He'd leave me there, straightening my clothes and I'd hear him speaking to them, saying, 'Come upstairs, to our bedroom.'

Just outside the door he'd stop them, poke his head round and say to me, 'We have visitors, darling,' and they'd squeeze in, sitting on the floor while Danny held court with me curled up beside him on the bed, my feet tucked under his legs. If they stayed too long, on a Sunday afternoon, for instance, he'd suddenly say to me, 'Ready for a nap, darling?' or announce to them that it was siesta time and he'd see them out while I lay back on the bed, cocooned in cigarette smoke, ready for him.

About a week after I'd come back from France, Cara phoned. It was her birthday that Saturday; I was so wrapped up in Danny that I'd almost forgotten, and I would have felt bad about that except it was so plainly obvious that she was only phoning me now as an afterthought. She was having some people round - or rather, '*Do you want to come round on Saturday night because Jacob and I are having a gathering?*'

A gathering, for God's sake! A gathering is what people have when they want to have a party and their parents won't let them. There'd be no smoking, there'd be no drinking and the parents would be in the other room, watching TV. And to hear her referring to Jacob and herself like they were an old married couple – did she not know how boring she made them sound?

Of course, not so long ago I'd have known about this gathering from the beginning. I'd have been in on the plans; I'd have known what she was going to wear, who she was going to invite, what music she'd play, right from the start. Now all I got was a last minute phone call, and grudging wasn't the word for it.

But I still replied, 'Oh right. Thanks. I'll ask Danny.'

And if she'd been frosty before, she went full-scale Arctic after that.

Danny didn't want to go. And it just didn't enter into it that I might go on my own. Danny didn't want to go, and he didn't want me to go.

He'd still got this thing in his head, about me and Jacob. Looking back, I wonder if I liked it that he was so jealous, though there really wasn't anything to be jealous of. I wonder if I encouraged it, and I think I must have done. I liked the feeling of Danny closing in on me, the thrill of his hands on my shoulders, his face up against mine, blocking out my eyes. My heart would skip up a beat, making me breathe shallow and fast. You know someone loves you when they want to hold on to you so tight they leave bruises on your arms. When they tell you they'll kill anyone who dares to so much as look at you, kissing the words home so hard that you can't hardly breathe.

I didn't go to Cara's gathering but I got bruises all up my arms like polka dots where Danny's fingers had been, and a slightly swollen lip. I must have been partly to blame for that, surely?

So I didn't see Cara all summer, and to be honest, I didn't even think about her. I was just too wrapped up in Danny.

It got to be so that pretty well every night, whether I'd been out with him or not, he'd be sitting outside my house on that wall opposite, when I went to bed. If I hadn't been out with Danny I'd have been out with no one; maybe he was checking up on me, maybe it was just love that had him there, a sort of goodnight.

That's how I want to think of it, like the sweetest goodnight.

* * *

128

We went up to London one day, on the train. The only time I'd ever been to London before was on school trips to museums but Danny seemed to know where to go. We got the tube to Oxford Circus and wandered our way up and down among the tourists and the pick-pockets till Danny took us down a little side road off to the right and instantly we were away from all that noise and came into this square, with a sort of garden in the middle of it. Golden Square, it was called – something like that, something dead romantic. We sat on a bench for a while, kissing, with the heat of the sun beating down on us and the dusty air drying in our eyes. We would have sat there for longer but there was a tramp shuffling about the place and he came right up by us, poking about in the bin by our bench. Then he sat down, right next to Danny and the stink of him had us up and away from there, double-quick, choking, laughing behind our hands.

You could weave your way for miles through those narrow streets and alleyways and we did, doubling back and forth on ourselves but not caring. We ended up in the streets round the back of Soho; there was this one road that had a fruit market from end to end. The smell of it in the heat was rank and they'd thrown water down onto the pavement to clear the mulch; I could feel it splashing up as I walked, getting inside my sandals and making my feet slide around. There were a couple of dodgy-looking strip clubs, just near the market. Danny said that years ago there used to be loads round there, and he said the tired old women you could see dragging themselves round the market would have been whores, once. We stopped and got a Coke in a little café; the guy behind the counter was Greek or something but there was this old woman in there with dyed-black hair scraped back in a knot on the top of her head, wiping tables and singing along to the radio. She was an ex-whore, too, Danny said; you could tell that by the bruises on the backs of her legs, where the veins stood out.

He got me a present; a tiny little pill box with an enamel lid. He nicked it from this weird shop near Leicester Square, a sprawling Aladdin's cave of a place crammed with nick-nacks and dope pipes and stinking of incense. Just slipped it in his pocket. The guy at the desk was too spaced out to even notice.

Everything seemed so romantic, even the guy dossing down outside the station with *spare any change* scribbled on a piece of cardboard, and propped against his knees.

'There you go, mate,' Danny said and he bunged him a cigarette as well as what little change he had left in his pocket.

'Cheers, mate,' the guy said, and he looked up at us and there was that connection, that thought

130

that it could be us, one day, getting out, any way you can, just getting out. All of this, it was just so far away from Eppingham.

On the train on the way home Danny put his arm around me and I laid my head against his shoulder, pretending to be asleep because I wanted to hold on to it all, to keep it all in my head, precious, unbroken.

I've still got that pill box. It's hidden inside a sock in the back of my drawer, and inside it there's a little lump of dope wrapped up in foil like a chip off an old Oxo cube, slowly rotting away. My own secret supply, my route to oblivion or hell or wherever it was that Danny went when I couldn't find him.

I knew he was taking too many drugs. I bumped into him in the street once, early one evening on a day when I hadn't seen him because I'd had to go out with my parents; when we got back my mum sent me round the corner to the shop to get some bread or something and I saw him, on the other side of the road, walking along. I called out but he didn't hear me, so I ran across.

'Danny!' I called but he looked at me, blank-faced for a second. Almost like he couldn't see me, even though he was looking right at me. Nothing registered, and that was so creepy. His eyes were like you'd imagine the eyes on a sleepwalker to be, open but not there. But the thing that shocked me most was the colour of his skin. I know he'd caught the sun a bit and everything but this was different, this was yellow.

He was going round with Mikey a lot more now, and no prizes for guessing why. Mikey had direct access to Bez, and God how they talked about him all the time, in this kind of hushed, reverential way.

It was all, 'Have you seen Bez?' and Mikey would have to think about that one, like it needed special thought. He'd try and keep his body still, though there'd be a twitch working its way out somewhere, through his foot, his leg, or the flicker above his eye.

'Yeah, the other night,' he'd say, drawing on his cigarette through restless fingers as he mulled it over. 'I saw him the other night.'

'Right,' Danny would say, and he'd nod his head as if this was actually some kind of proper conversation they were having.

Sometimes it would end there, but sometimes Mikey would say something like, 'He said he'd be down The Riverside on Friday. Thought I might try and get in.' And then they'd go on, like either of them ever stood a hope in hell of getting past the bouncer who guarded the door of The Riverside. The car park was as far as they'd get and they knew it.

It got on my nerves.

* * *

Still, no matter what he did at night, no matter where he went, he'd come by my house, sooner or later. Sometimes I'd have been asleep and then I'd wake up, wide awake, sudden, with my heart rattling loose, and I'd get up, and I'd look out my window, and there he'd be. Sat on that wall, almost hidden in the darkness by the greater darkness of that tree.

Even in sleep I knew he was there. He was in my head, in my dreams. I couldn't have escaped, even if I wanted to.

9

The night before we went back to school Danny bought a bottle of vodka and we went to the boathouse, and made love and it felt like an ending, like goodbye. I was crying as he kissed me, drunk I suppose, more than anything but if I could have stopped things right then I would have done. I stared up at the sky and I couldn't tell if it was us or the stars, spinning round and round, out of control. Like those toys you get when you're a kid that you press down on with your thumb then let go to have them spinning faster and faster, whizzing out lights and that weird, high-pitched shriek that whirrs up louder with the speed. And then you can press back down again to have it stop, instant. That was like us, and I'd have done that, I'd have pressed down my thumb.

Better that than to ever have to watch it slow down, and fizzle out.

In the morning he didn't meet me. Our first day back at school and I walked on my own, with a lump the size of a fist in my heart.

In the corridors, in the form room, everyone else was

chattering away so loud it was like a scream; *Hi, hello, What did you do? We did this, We did that*, going on and on. I hid myself in it. After all, what had I done all summer? I'd given myself to Danny, that's all, and now Danny wasn't even here.

Then when I came out at half-three Richard was waiting for me. Had I heard from Danny, he said, did I know where he was?

I hadn't and I didn't, and there was a deep coldness turning over inside me.

'He had a fight with his mum,' Richard said, dark eyes split narrow in the sun. 'Last night. She phoned me up, this morning. Said he hit her, hit his sister and he ran off. She was dead worried,' he said. 'Said he went mental.'

In spite of the heat I could feel my teeth starting to chatter.

'He won't answer his phone. And his mum don't know where he is.' He shrugged his shoulders and at the same time blew the hair out of his eyes; he'd got little eyes and there was a frown, cut sharp between them. 'I haven't seen him,' he said. 'What about you? D'you know where he could be?'

Of course I knew where he'd be, if no one else did. He'd be at the boathouse. But I wasn't going to tell Richard that, or anyone. No one even knew it existed, apart from Danny and me. And the old guy who lived in the big house, I suppose.

I tried Danny's phone but he didn't answer. So I had no choice. I had to go there, after school. He'd be waiting for me.

I'd never been there on my own before. I crept my way through the reeds, terrified I'd slip and sink, and then on through the brambles, lugging my school bag behind me. I had to remember the way and stick to it; that wire fence ran all the way round the house but I had to be sure to get to the right bit or I could end up anywhere. I stared across the grass before I ran, waiting for that dog to bark; Jesus, I was scared. It could be loose in the grounds for all I knew and it seemed a hell of a long way to the other side. This was some kind of mission I was on, some kind of test; it had to be. If I hesitated a second longer I wouldn't be able to do it at all so I ran for it, as fast as I ever could across that lawn and God did that dog bark; I could picture it, straining against its leash, breaking free. And I could feel that old man in the house, at one of those windows, watching me, I was sure I could. He had to know about us, of course he did.

My heart was hammering so hard I felt sick and I practically threw myself over the fence on the other side, scraping the skin right off my leg above my knee. Now I was crying; I was thinking what if I was wrong, what if he wasn't here? I'd got to get back yet, somehow. And I was thinking, what if I took a wrong turn? I could die out here and no one would know.

But Danny was there, sat on the step outside the boathouse, and he was waiting for me. I cried even more when I saw him, out of relief more than anything. At least I wouldn't have to go all that way back, on my own. And if this was a test, I'd passed it, surely? At first I couldn't even speak; I sat down beside him and he put his arm around my shoulder, stroking me, comforting me. Did I ever feel so much that it was just me and him against whatever it was in the world that he thought was choking us?

'You've got to go back, Danny,' I said. It was nearly five; I'd phoned my mum and said I was going to be late but I couldn't be *that* late. After I'd spoken to her I'd switched off my phone. She'd be sitting at the kitchen table, watching the clock, imagining all sorts. 'You can't stay here. You've got nothing to eat, nothing to drink.'

He shrugged. 'I don't need anything.'

'But you do. And your mum's worried. Everyone's worried. No one knew where you were.'

'You knew,' Danny said, holding me close; I could smell his skin, the acid smell of all night, here, by the river, clinging to him. 'And I don't care about anyone else.' He kissed me and his mouth was tobacco-coated and dry. I wanted to pull away but how could I? 'I'm never going back,' he said at last but he was, of course; he had to. We both knew that.

I could feel the air cooling around us. I thought of my mother, probably pacing the room now, biting at her lips. What on earth was I going to tell her, to get out of this? That my watch had stopped? She'd probably got a search party out by now.

'I've got to get back, Danny,' I said. 'We both have.'

'Do you know what the worst thing was?' he said. 'While I was sitting here, I had time to think, you know, about us, about everything. And the worst thing was just going back to school. I couldn't do it. I couldn't go back to that place and see you in the distance again, so far away from me.'

'I'm not far away from you. I'm here.'

'You know what I mean,' he said, and then he said those desperate, dreaded words that I hadn't heard once, all summer: 'You're too good for me, Louise.'

And the awful thing was, it didn't break my heart the way it used to.

He started talking then about how we'd run away, soon. We'd go to London. No, better than that, we'd sneak our passports out of the house and go to New York, to this place he'd heard of called Times Square, a place that was full of people like us, getting out. We'd get our tickets on the internet, you could get them dead cheap if you shopped around; we'd do it soon, dead soon. He talked all the way back, pausing only for the time it took us to run the distance in front of the big house and then he carried on again, out of breath but so determined, so much to say.

I let it all wash over me. I so, so wanted to believe it all, back then.

My mother was doing her nut with me back so late, but it was Mrs Crosby I saw first. I swear she was out the front, waiting for me. She was pretending to pick at her roses but you don't get a gleam like that in your eye over pruning your flowers.

I heard her click her tongue against her teeth, otherwise I might have missed her. But catching my eye she couldn't help herself but to peer over that rose bush and say, 'Oh your mother's been out of her mind, young lady, wondering where you were.'

Mealy-mouthed old witch. She's the first person I wouldn't miss, if ever I did get away.

'Where've you been?' my mum yelled the minute I opened the door. I was prepared for this, but even so it didn't make it any easier. The kitchen was in chaos. There was broccoli, cooked and strewn across the floor, pan and sieve up-ended, and my mum was dripping all down the front of her in what I thought was blood and then I realised it was tomatoes, out of a tin. 'It's nearly six o'clock. What have you been doing?'

'I phoned you,' I said, dead calm, because dead calm was the only way to say anything to my mother, though I didn't feel it, not one bit. I mean God, did I have to come home to this, after everything else?

'You phoned me nearly two hours ago,' she shrieked and spit bubbled up and caught on her lip. 'I've been calling you and calling you—' She picked up the phone and shook it at me and tomato gloop slid off her fingers and onto the keys. The phone got slippery and she dropped it, onto the mess beside the sink; the dirty dishes, the chopped and abandoned meat, the wine bottle. Oh yes of course, the empty wine bottle. 'But you turned off your phone.' She said it like it was the worst thing. She said it like it hurt.

My God, if only I could just turn *her* off.

'No I didn't,' I lied, pitching my eyes on the tomatoes spewed down her front instead of on her hunted-rabbit eyes. 'You must have misdialled. Or maybe there was no signal. I had my phone on all the time.' I got it out my bag, now, to prove it. I'd turned it back on before I got home, of course, but she wouldn't think of that, she didn't have the brains. 'I've been watching the football like I told you,' I said. 'Down in the park. Danny was playing. His team won, three nil.'

Danny's mum was going out with her friend Dawn and we were babysitting.

We were sat on the sofa. Danny's mum and Dawn had sat, one in the chair and one on its arm, both of them squeezed into too-tight black trousers and frilly tops, drinking gins and giggling like a couple of girls while they waited for the taxi. Ellie was on the floor in her pyjamas, bum in the air, watching a quiz show on TV.

The second Danny's mum and Dawn were gone Danny turned off the TV, and said, 'Go to bed, Ellie, or I'll break your fucking neck.'

Ellie sat up, and looked from Danny to me, tears piling up. I smiled sympathetically at her, to soften Danny's words.

'Shall I come up in a minute?' I said. 'And tuck you up?'

And Ellie, still hovering on tears, nodded.

We'd have the whole evening to ourselves, two hours, undisturbed before I had to go home. No way would Ellie come back downstairs after Danny had spoken to her like that.

But Mikey came round. If it had been anyone else,

turning up when Danny and I had got the house to ourselves, they'd have been sent away again, straight away. But because it was Mikey, he stood there, talking. And I heard what he said. He said, 'No I can't, mate, I've got Louise here. Got a job to do. Come back later.'

In October we had to get our applications in for college. I was going to just put down the Sixth Form in Swanley but Miss Reynolds my art teacher caught me at the end of a lesson and said, 'Have you thought of applying to Meadlands? They have a much better art department. Think about it. You're good enough. You could go far if you work hard.'

I told Danny when I went round his house that night, and suddenly there was this divide between us.

There was never any question of me not going to college. Apart from anything else it was a route out. And Meadlands College even more so. I could just see myself, away from Cara and everyone else with their petty little minds, away from school rules.

'I don't want you to go,' Danny said, and that black cloud came down.

'Why not? I've got to go somewhere.' He was staring at me, mouth tight, and with that darkness in his eyes. I should have seen it. 'We'll still be together,' I said easily enough but did I mean it? Did I *really* mean it?

'You're not going,' he said.

I almost laughed. Who did he think he was to tell me not to go to college? In my head I was there already, I was *gone*. He saw it on my face. He saw it, and slapped it out. His hand burned against my cheek, knocking back my head, hard. For seconds I couldn't breathe, I couldn't even see. I could feel the side of my face melting, and ballooning out.

And then *he* was the one crying, yanking me into his arms, pinning me against his chest so tight I still couldn't breathe.

'I love you,' he said into my hair. 'You know I love you. Don't do this to me. Don't destroy us. Please, I can't let you go.' And he kept on saying all this stuff, over and over, gripping me like a rag doll. Till eventually he loosened his grip, and immediately I started shaking. There was this voice in my head saying, *get out, get out* and yet I sat there as he kissed my face where he'd hit me, and I listened as he told me how much he loved me and that he would never, ever hurt me again. Sat there like I was powerless. I couldn't even think, for the love and the pain swimming around inside my head.

I shouted goodnight to my parents and went straight up to my room. I didn't turn my light on. I didn't want Danny to see me. He was sat outside my house, on that wall. I couldn't even draw the curtains or he'd see me, moving. I just wanted to be alone, totally alone.

I sat on my bed and peered at my face in my hand-mirror. Even in just the moonlight I could see the bruise starting up. I felt in my chest the way you feel when you've run too far, too fast. Tight, packed out. There were so many tears inside my head I was afraid to let them out.

How could this happen to me? You think of women who let themselves get hit, you think of *victims*.

How could it be that love and pain could be so mixed up, could feel so much the same?

I shut my eyes and lay back on my bed. The tears were boiling up and spilling out, running sideways into my hair.

He was texting me, again and again. Every couple of seconds my phone bleeped. I knew it was him. Who else would it be? And I knew what he'd be saying. He'd be saying he loved me, he was sorry, did I forgive him; the same old stuff.

Once, when my granny was in one of her wisdom-spouting moods, she said to me, 'Love, Louise, is a very special thing. Often you might think yourself in love but when you find the right man, you'll know for sure. I knew it the minute I met your grandad, and you will too. It's like they've got your soul.' I laughed at the time, of course. My granny's always talking romantic nonsense. But now I could see what she meant.

Danny had got my soul all right. And now it was black and damned to hell.

Next morning the bruise was like a shadow beside my eye. I hid it from my mum well enough, just kept my head down and let my hair fall over my face. I knew she hated that. She said it made me look sullen. I ate my toast and I could feel her watching me, plotting her attack. She clattered her spoon against her cup. She picked the cup up. She put it down again.

Please don't, I willed inside my head. *Not today. Please don't.*

'You're very quiet this morning,' she accused and then in an instant her voice changed, became all knowing, all pally-pally and blanket-thick. 'Boyfriend trouble?'

I shrugged, keeping my head dipped down, and away from her.

'You can talk to me, you know,' she gushed, as if she actually meant it.

In spite of myself I could feel the tears banking up again, and I bit on the inside of my lip to control them.

Talk to her? As if I ever could.

* * *

Jacob was in my art class. He didn't talk to me much these days but we'd just started on a new composition, and we were working in groups, and he was in mine.

He couldn't not talk to me, and suddenly I remembered what it was like when we used to be friends, when we hung around together all the time. And I realised I'd missed him. I missed those times, those times before Danny, before everything had got so complicated. It all seemed so long ago, like from another life. So *innocent*.

I might have been going out with Jacob, now, if things had been different.

Instead of that, he was going out with Cara. Curiously, I wondered if they'd done it. Would that make us the same now, Cara and me, if they had? I bet Jacob didn't hit her when he got mad. I bet he didn't even get mad.

'How's Cara?' I asked him, because I'd never get to ask her that these days. Emma had taken my place in the favourite friend stakes, well and truly.

'She's fine,' Jacob said, kind of off-hand, and he went a little pink. Now why would that be? I'd caught him looking at me, often, when he should have been looking at his work.

I was thinking how he'd always fancied me more than Cara, and that maybe I'd been wrong to let him go. And that maybe, just maybe, if Danny and me split up, then maybe . . . I was running along in my head, thinking all these things when suddenly Jacob said, 'What happened to your face?'

Heat shot up the sides of my head into my ears. Heat, *shame*. I always stuck my hair behind my ears when I was painting. I'd forgotten about that bruise.

'Did Danny do that to you?'

The thing is, I could hear the contempt in his voice. The disgust. And that was worse than anything. Forget any notions about Jacob fancying me. He thought I was a *fool*. I couldn't think what to say. I unhooked the hair off my ear, too late. But believe me, if Jacob hated me right then, I hated myself a whole lot more.

'You're stupid, going out with that creep,' Jacob said, and I couldn't look at him any more, couldn't bear the way *he* was looking at me. I dipped my head and a tear dropped onto my picture, and another; they were racing out. Vaguely, I heard him tut, but that was all. I just sat there, with my head over my work, quietly crying my eyes out till the bell went, and then I was out of that studio, fast. I didn't even know Jacob had followed me till he put his hand on my arm, and caught me.

'Wait,' he said, and there was concern in his voice now, and that had me crying harder. He pulled me into his arms, holding my head against his shoulder, right there in the corridor. And it was just the nicest place to be. 'Don't cry,' he said. 'It'll be all right.'

But somebody must have seen us, and told Danny.

When I came out of school at three-thirty there was a crowd gathered outside the gates. I don't know how but I knew Danny was there, in the centre somewhere. Maybe it was the way people were looking at me, I don't know, but there was a chill creeping out on my skin. I ran over, pushed my way through; Danny had got Jacob pinned against the wall and he was pummelling the hell out of him.

I ran in there, screaming for him to stop, got myself a fist in the chest, fell back, got in there again.

'Stop it, Danny! Just stop it!' I got hold of his arm and clung on, tight, so he couldn't shake me off. Jacob's lip was bleeding; I saw it and my heart split.

Behind me I heard someone shout, 'Walker's coming!' and the crowd diminished and Danny pulled back, reluctant, breathing hard.

Jacob wiped his hand across his face, and spat on the ground. He looked at me, and I never want to have anyone look at me that way again.

'Your boyfriend's a fucking nutter,' he said, dragging himself away from that wall, and those were the last words he said to me, ever.

'He's not my boyfriend!' I yelled up the road after him. 'Not any more.' And I would have gone after him, I swear I would have but Danny grabbed hold of my wrist, twisting the skin, and yanked me along with him, up the alleyway, fast; Mr Walker was at the gates, looking for trouble, hoping there was none.

'What do you mean by that?' Danny hissed into my face once we were up that alley, alone, away from prying eyes, and now it was me, pinned against the wall. But I wasn't scared. Not now.

'I'm not going out with you any more. Not after that.'

'I did it for you,' Danny said, and he shook me. He was pressed up close against me; I could feel his breath on my face and his heart, thumping its way out of his body and into mine. 'You don't want that creep trying it on, do you? Do you?'

He shook me again but it wasn't anger now, it was desperation; I could see it in his eyes.

'He wasn't trying it on. He was being nice to me, that's all.'

'That's not the way I heard it.'

'Well tell your spies to get their facts right next time.' He was staring at me so hard I felt like he could see inside my head. I tried to look away but he grabbed my chin, yanking me back. 'For God's sake, Danny, you can't go around hitting everyone who talks to me.'

'He had you in his fucking arms. Is that what you wanted, then? Is it?'

I had wanted it, hadn't I? I shook my head but I was guilty. Danny knew it, I knew it. It was my fault he'd smacked Jacob. All of this, my fault.

'What are you doing to me, Louise?' he said, pleading with me now; I could hear the hurt in him, wrenching itself out. His grip on my arms loosened and tightened again, loosened and tightened, and there were tears brimming up in his eyes. How could it be me causing all this pain?

'I can't stand this, Danny,' I said and I was crying too. 'I just can't stand it.'

I pushed away from him and started running away up the alley, out towards the road. For a moment I thought he was going to let me go, but then suddenly he was running up behind me, chasing me. When he caught me he didn't stop me but half pushed, half pulled me out into the road with him so that a car had to screech its breaks and swerve to miss us and I screamed at him, screamed *You're going to kill us* but I don't think he cared and by then I didn't really either. On the other side of the road there was a grass verge and we fell down, both of us, holding on to each other, clinging on.

My heart was running away, out of control, and inside my head I'd gone to the peak, up, up, could go no higher. He was kissing me hard and I kissed him back; I could taste the tears running into my mouth. His tears, mine, I don't know.

'You nearly killed me,' I said when I could breathe again and Danny put his forehead against mine, eyes shut, just holding me close.

'No, it's you,' he whispered. 'It's you who's killing me.'

10

You could have frozen hell with the look Cara gave me at school the next day. And she huddled herself up with Emma, who just revelled in all this. Every time I saw them (and I tried not to) Emma'd got her fat arms all around Cara, protecting her from the likes of me.

You'd think it had been me that hit Jacob.

Jacob sat in art with his swollen lips clamped shut. It made me miserable as hell to think it was my fault this had all happened, and I did say sorry. I said it the first chance I got, the first time I saw him again in art. And in a way, we both had something in common now; we'd both been hit by Danny. Stupidly, I thought there might be some connection in that.

'God, I am so sorry, Jacob,' I said.

He looked at me, saying nothing, and looked away again. He didn't want to know.

And you should have seen them, him and Cara, going around together with their arms stuck around each others' waists. Sometimes I watched them across the playground and I wondered what they had to talk about, apart from me of course. Seeing them there, both with their blonde hair, all squeaky clean, I realised I could never be like them again. I'd gone beyond that. I'd be bored in seconds.

And at least Danny wasn't boring. At least with Danny you really knew you were alive. He was like a coin, held up to the sun, and turned, bright and shade, bright and shade, revolving.

It was just the drugs that fucked him up, and took him away from me.

He didn't want to let me out of his sight. He walked me to school, he walked me back again. Even if he didn't actually go into school himself, he usually still walked with me. And if he didn't do that, he'd have his friends watching out for me. I felt like I was being guarded. Everyone else, keep off. That message was going out, loud and clear.

I tried not to mind. I mean, doesn't everyone want to be loved that much? The way the other girls looked at me – wasn't that just jealousy?

Wasn't it?

No boys looked at me at all now, of course, unless they wanted to get thumped.

I was on an island, cut out.

Sometimes when I did get to walk home from school

on my own I'd find myself taking a detour past Natalie's old house. It felt sneaky, doing that. I'd have the shivers going up and down my spine for the short distance along the main road between the turn off for my road, and Fairview Drive, where Natalie used to live. I'd walk quick, the whole back of me tense with the fear of being watched, followed, *found out*. God, you'd think I was doing something wrong, the way I felt. I'd only feel like I'd got away with it once I was a good way down Fairview Drive, which is a shortish, quietish road with only a handful of houses, hardly any cars, and nowhere to hide but that meant if anyone was following me *they* couldn't hide either.

And then I'd just kind of loiter, flooding myself with memories of Natalie and me. I used to do this a lot, after she died. Not immediately after because at first I was too freaked out, after that first time I'd come round, and her brother had told me she was dead. But when I heard her dad had moved away I eventually plucked up the courage to come down here again, to see her house. I had to do it, to know she wasn't totally gone. I remember I was terrified, thinking I'd see her ghost standing outside her house, and then when I didn't, I *wanted* to. So I sort of *willed* her back. I let my eyes half close so my vision blurred and I concentrated and concentrated so hard that I could see her, see her so clear, in and outside of my head, running around, laughing, talking to me.

It made her not so gone.

Here I was, doing that again, now. I could see her, small, skinny, skinnier than me, wearing her jeans of course, and her straight brown hair hanging in her eyes, hair always a bit greasy – my mum always said she looked like she needed a good bath – but what did we care about things like that, back then? I could see her eyes, so bright and alive, always thinking up something, some plan, some scheme.

She had a dog, a black one, quite big, don't know what sort, called Jasper, and we used to take him for walks, just up and down her road. Natalie had a pair of pink and gold sandals with heels and she let me wear them, to walk the dog, even though they were at least a size too small. They had a huge TV in their front room; I remember when they got it, and when the big satellite disc went up on their roof and you could get cartoons, all day. They'd all watch TV together, even in the daytime, her mum and dad sat on the sofa, brother in the chair and Natalie and me on the floor with the dog. It was the cosiest place to be, on a Saturday afternoon. I wished that we could get a TV like theirs but when I said that to my mum she went off on one of her anti-Natalie rants, saying that people like them ought to know better than to waste their money on such things.

Natalie's skin smelt of butter. Once we were hiding in the grass at the end of her garden, spying on the boys next door. They heard us and we ducked down, huddled together; my face fell on Natalie's arm. Butter, left out in the sun.

I remember all these things but what's the use in remembering? I wish I had her here now, to talk to.

'I want to go to Meadlands,' I blurted out, into the mind-numbing silence of our happy family mealtime. I'd wanted it to come out strong, decisive, but I could hear myself sounding petulant, like I actually wanted the inevitable argument that would follow. And really, I'd only said it then because somebody had to say *something*, before the silence did my head in.

I stared at my plate while my parents stared at me. I didn't want to eat. I wanted to *get out*.

'Meadlands,' my dad repeated, reasonable man that he is. 'I see.' I still stared at my plate but I could see them anyway, shadows at the sides of my eyes, my dad nodding his head, mulling it over, my mum, hissing herself up into a fit. 'That's quite some distance.'

'Some distance?' my mum snapped, letting fly right out with the histrionics. It was like there was a button in her, and I never failed to hit it, every time. 'It's ten miles away at least. Meadlands! How on earth do you think you'll get there every day?'

'I can get the bus to Swanley and the train from there.'

I may as well not have spoken.

'And what do you want to go to Meadlands for when there's a perfectly good Sixth Form right here in Eppingham?'

'It isn't right here in Eppingham. It's in Swanley. I'd have to get the bus there.'

'Don't pick hairs with me. Swanley is five minutes away. Meadlands is – is—'

'It's totally different to Swanley. It's got a fantastic art department.'

'How would you know? You haven't even been there.'

I looked at her now; her face was all a-twitch, eyes, nose, mouth, all frantically working against each other. 'I've heard about it. Miss Reynolds told me. And she said I'm good enough.' There: eat your way out of that one. I'm good enough, me, Louise, the long streak of nothing. I knew my mum would put up all these obstacles, all these reasons why I shouldn't go there. I knew she would do her damnedest to put me down, but even so I couldn't deal with it. There was a blood-red haze, fizzing up the sides of my head.

'Art, art, art,' my mum said, huffing up her shoulders

and pulling her cardigan close, across her chest, like she could keep the madness out with the cold. 'When are you ever going to snap out of all this *art*?'

'Never. It's all I want to do.'

'It's that boy, putting ideas into your head.'

'It's not! God, you're just like him. You're all the same, all of you, trying to stop me doing what I want to do!'

'How can you possibly know what you want to do? You're fifteen years old. You're a child.'

I laughed. It came out like a snarl. 'I know I don't want to be like you.'

She glared at me like she hated me. I glared back, and believe me, I really did hate her, right then. 'Fifteen years of my life I've given up for you. Fifteen, and more. All those stupid, wasted years trying, praying for a baby. And what did I get?'

'Now then, Gillian,' my dad said, Mr Steady-On Nice-Guy. 'Let's all calm down.'

No one took any notice.

'I got you. And your bloody ingratitude.' She was blubbering up now, thin tears streaking their way down the sides of her nose. How bad did she want to make me feel? 'I gave up my life for you.'

'Well I wish you hadn't.'

She closed her eyes like I'd hurt her but she was the

one hurting me. Didn't she know it? Didn't she know what it feels like to know how *unwanted* you are? But on and on it goes, this battle that we have had so many times before, and so many times since. She wants me, she doesn't want me; and me, all I want to do is get away.

And what did my father do to defuse this particular outburst of mother-daughter hate?

He slunk off out to the kitchen, and started putting out the bins.

I wish it didn't upset me. I wish I could wipe my mother out of my head. What is it they say? That hate is just the other side of love? How can I ever know if that's true when they both feel pretty much the same to me?

'We'll go away. Soon,' Danny said, stroking the hair away from my face. He was sitting with his back against the wall of the boathouse and I was lying, curled up because there wasn't much room, with my head in his lap. He'd wrapped me up in his jacket but I was still freezing. He stroked his hand in time to the words he said, comforting, soothing. 'They'll all miss us when we're gone. We don't need them. We don't need any of this shit. I'll get our tickets then, soon. I'll get them off the internet. It'll be all right once we're there. I can easily pass for eighteen. We both can. We'll get through all right. You just got to show your passport, quick . . .'

His hand stilled on my head, fingers tense, catching dreams. But that's all they were, dreams.

I closed my eyes, letting his words lull me. I so, so wished I could believe him.

I was leaning out my bedroom window, having a fag. The parents were downstairs, stuck in front of the TV for the evening. They wouldn't come up. I stuck my head right out, into the dark. It was raining; it had been raining all day. That soft, persistent rain that weighs the whole world down. I listened to it pattering into the gutter above my head and running down. I puffed out the smoke and it fogged up around me, trapped by all that damp.

I'd put in my application for Meadlands.

I didn't tell Danny. I didn't tell my mum and dad, though I knew they wouldn't stop me now, for all my mum's banging on.

I told Miss Reynolds, though. She stopped me in the corridor; she'd looked out for me, specially, because I didn't do art on a Thursday.

'Good, good,' she said when I told her. And she did the weirdest thing. She put her hand on my arm. 'Don't waste yourself, Louise. Don't let other people . . . keep you back.'

I drew hard on my cigarette and the nib hissed and burned. All Danny's talk about running away was just that: talk. Fantasy. We couldn't run away. Not really. Where would we live? What would we do?

I'd got myself a real way out. There was no way I wasn't going to take it.

Suddenly I heard something, out in the dark. I looked down, and there was Mrs Crosby, staring right back up at me. Shit! I stubbed out my cigarette on the window sill and held the butt in my hand. Too late to shut the window.

She was calling to her cat. She must have come out from the back and I hadn't heard. 'Here, Sasha,' she called but she was looking at me. I could see the glee in her eyes even from that distance, and in the dark. I pulled back into my room, but she'd seen me all right, and she'd seen my cigarette.

No doubt about it.

It took till next day when I got home from school for all hell to break loose.

I saw Mrs Crosby poking about in her porch next door when I walked up our path, and I just knew she'd told my mum. She was probably round there first thing, the minute I'd left for school.

I went round the back, braced myself, and walked into the onslaught.

My mum had been sitting at the kitchen table but she leapt up as soon as I opened the door, and started ranting at me. Screwed up tissues flew off her lap as she stood up, fluttering like blossom down onto the floor to be trampled under her bare feet. She was still in her dressing-gown. It was belted tight at the middle but gaping open over her nightie and you could see her breasts, just hanging there behind the thin nylon. They swung about as she stamped around the kitchen, beating her hands at the air. She'd got an anger rash burning up from her chest into her neck and I could smell her warm, waxy smell. I tried to keep the disgust off my face. I tried to stay calm, blanked-out as she yelled that I was bad, deceitful, a liar, a slut, a tart and God knows what else. When someone screams at you like that it doesn't matter what they're saying; all you hear is the hate.

My dad was there; vaguely I noticed him in the background, summoned home from work early to witness the drama. Or was it to chastise me? I don't know, because all he seemed to be doing was shadowing my mum as she flung herself about the room. His arms would go up and down, up and down, as if he had in his hands an imaginary net with which to catch her, and he kept saying *calm down now, let's talk about this properly* and all those other useless things that nobody ever took any notice of.

She'd got the evidence. It was there on the table. A box of matches. She picked it up and threw it at me and I moved away too slow; it hit me just above my eye and flew open, scattering matches all over the tiles.

'Don't you deny it, my girl!' she hissed at me, but I hadn't been going to. She must have really hunted through my room to find those matches because I'd certainly forgotten they were there. And I was thinking thank God it was only a box of matches she'd found and not the little lump of dope stashed in the pill box. Imagine how she'd have reacted *then*.

'It's that boy,' she snapped.

'No it's not.'

'It's his fault.'

'How can it be his fault? It's nothing to do with him.'

'He got you into this.'

'I do have a mind of my own.'

'Don't get facetious with me, young lady. I know what you're up to. You and that boy.'

I laughed. I mean, what were we talking about now? Smoking? *Sex?* Or what?

Suddenly her hand shot out and caught me a slap on the side of my face. It didn't really hurt; she was shaking too much to aim well and nearly missed altogether, and let's face it, I've had worse. But even so.

'I hate you,' I said and the words burned my throat.

Her nose and her mouth were twitching like mad. She'd stuck her teeth into her lip and it was bleeding. She looked like she was going to explode.

Behind me I could hear my dad saying, 'Now, now, let's not get silly.' Or something equally useless.

'You'll stop seeing that boy.'

'No I won't.'

'Oh yes you will.'

'You can't make me.'

'Oh yes I can, my girl.'

'And how are you going to do that? Are you going to lock me up? Or are you going to hit me again?'

For a second I thought she *was* going to hit me again but then she seemed to deflate. She sort of sagged in on herself. She'd burned herself out, for now.

But the issue was still there. That wasn't going away. Not until I stopped smoking and stopped seeing Danny. Chances were I'd end up doing both one day, but not to please her. I was long past ever doing anything to please her.

They didn't stop me going out but they puffed themselves right up every time I did, putting all these obstacles in my way. It was all 'Have you done your homework, have you cleaned your room, cleaned the bathroom, ironed your clothes?' – and done all the other fifty million chores that were suddenly manifested in order to try and keep me in. And when I eventually did get out my dad would tap his watch, demanding that I be home at some ridiculously early hour while my mum sat chewing at her lips and her nails, looking like she was about to have a fit of the vapours over Danny, who would forever more be referred to only as *that boy*.

Sometimes I wondered if it was even worth it, going through all that hassle.

It had rained solidly for two weeks and Danny and I just went to Doug's most of the time, when we went out. We had no money for anything else. Sometimes Danny used to work at the pub down Field Lane, helping stock up the barrels, but any money he got he just spent on dope. And my parents had stopped my pocket money, so I couldn't go spending it on cigarettes. I wanted to get a job, on Saturdays, in a shop or something but that just drove Danny off into a mood, saying other guys would be after me all the time, coming into the baker's or the newsagent or wherever it was to get a look at me, and was that what I wanted? Was it?

I couldn't be bothered to argue.

So we had no money, and nothing to do, except talk about *one day, one day* all the time.

We even went to Doug's on my birthday. My birthday was on a Friday, at the end of October. I got the most unheartfelt 'Happy Birthday' ever from my mum and dad, and vouchers, because at least vouchers couldn't be spent on cigarettes. Danny called for me in the evening, and out we went, into the rain. The air was a great dark, wet weight, weighing us down. Just round the corner from my house we stopped where there was this great tree hanging over a wall, and huddled up, trying to shelter from the rain, and I opened my present. He'd got me a ring, silver with a glass stone in it, like a diamond. He took my left hand and put it on my wedding finger. And that was where he wanted me to wear it, he said, when we were out and when we were alone, as the friendship ring was too big.

'I'll get you a proper one soon,' he said and I felt this overwhelming sadness, pressing down on me. Weak, lazy tears drizzled their way out and he followed them down my face with his finger. 'It's OK,' he said, putting his arms around me and pulling me close so that I was held, safe but not safe, breathing in that scent, that precious, never-to-be-forgotten scent, of leather and tobacco, of Danny.

He bought us a bottle of vodka, as it was my birthday.

He'd nicked the money from his mum's purse but he said she'd never notice and if she did he'd just deny it. Then we sat on Doug's bed, and drank it. All of it. But it didn't take me far enough out of myself. Nothing would any more.

I could feel Danny's ring on my finger. It didn't fit that well; it was too tight and I'd have to get it off later, when I went home.

It was my birthday and yet I felt the most miserable I'd ever felt in my life.

Didn't I want more than anything to be with Danny, forever? And yet there was this turning feeling inside of me, despair, like you're running at a wall. You're going to hit it soon.

I was just sixteen, yet I felt like I'd lived my life already.

Mikey'd got some special stuff. I couldn't tell you what; I wasn't interested. Only whatever it was required equipment for cooking up and a special little spoon, though he had to make do with a teaspoon nicked from home. And we all had to troupe off to that place at the back of the old petrol station on Swanley Road to witness the importance of this stuff. That place that I thought Danny and I had come across by accident the night of the concert, way back when.

Whatever it was you cooked it up on looked like a mini version of my granny's kitchen scales to me, with a lighter held underneath. Mikey held the lighter, pressing so hard on the catch to light the flame that the tip of his finger bent out the wrong way, like he was double jointed. Only he wasn't, it was just that his hand shook too much to hold it any other way.

'It's all right,' Mikey said, looking right at me though I hadn't said anything. 'You don't get hooked if you only smoke it.'

No way was I going anywhere near the stuff. I sat there, shivering in the cold, while Danny, Richard and Mikey passed round this dodgy, foul-smelling joint. I wished I'd worn something warmer. I wished I could block out my ears to the things they were saying, to the *Wow man, that is good* and *Bez is great, Bez is the man* and all the other stupid, stupid things they were saying.

'Here, Louise,' Danny said, pointing that soggy joint at me, though I didn't take it. Not that he cared. He took another toke himself and toppled backwards, hitting his head on the concrete with a thump. He didn't even seem to notice. He was too busy laughing, at nothing. A stupid, high-pitched laugh that cracked right through me.

And suddenly I got this vision, this horrible, horrible vision of Danny in ten, twenty years' time, no job, no money, no hope. Like those old men you see on buses, with their nylon trousers and plastic shopping bags, or in the pub, propping up the bar till it closes. What else is there if you never get away and just smoke yourself into a hole?

I'd got myself an interview at Meadlands, though I hadn't told Danny. It had come in the post, that morning. And at school Miss Reynolds had told me she'd put in a recommendation for me. I was as good as there.

I put my head on my knees and started crying, and once I'd started I couldn't stop. Nobody noticed. They were all too out of it by then to even know I was there.

I knew it was over. I'd been rehearsing in my head the way to say it.

I was going to tell him, soon. It wasn't exactly that I was frightened, not really. Just that I had to pick the right moment.

But then something awful happened, just a few nights later.

Mikey Petes went and fell off the motorway bridge, and got himself killed.

11

It runs through my head like a nightmare on constant replay. Sometimes at night I have to have the light on and my bedside lamp and I lie there with my eyes wide open, staring to keep awake but it's still there in the back of my head, in the shadows. Ink on my brain; it never goes away.

We'd gone to the petrol station again, me, Danny, Richard and Mikey but this time no one had anything to smoke except the scraps that they grubbed around in their pockets for, tipping out the tiniest crumbs from screwed-up bits of old tin foil and cling film and mixing them all together. And no one had any money, either, to buy any drink or anything. So we just sat there while they smoked this one pathetic joint that wasn't worth the match that lit it, then worked their way through the last of Richard's cigarettes. I had this feeling like my head was being squeezed. I didn't want to be there any more. Didn't want to be doing this.

Everyone was in a weird mood. Even the weather was weird, with this annoying wind that ought to have been cold but was too warm instead and gusted about in all directions, getting under your hair and throwing up dirt into your eyes.

Danny was bent over on his knees and his elbows, shadowing a loose Rizla paper with his cupped hands as the wind flipped it around on the concrete so it looked like he'd got some invisible string attached to it, making it dance. And he had a look on his face like this was all he was going to do, all night. Mikey'd been sprawled out on his side watching Danny and suddenly he got on to his knees too, and shoved his face in front of Danny's.

'I'm bored,' he shouted, right in Danny's face. I'm 'B-O-R-E-D.' The word rang out on a crescendo, going on and on. I thought he'd never get to the D. Then the second he did Danny shot a hand out and thumped him in the mouth. Mikey flopped back onto the ground and lay staring at the sky. 'I'm *bored*,' he said in a whisper this time, like he was pleading with the stars.

I looked at Danny, who just carried on playing with that paper again, and at Richard, who was dismantling his empty cigarette packet and rolling up what he could of it into roaches, which he lined up on his knee. And I wondered how we ever thought any of this was fun.

Suddenly Danny snapped his head up. 'We'll go to Doug's,' he said. 'Get some money off him.'

'Doug's not going to give us his money,' Richard muttered but there's no reasoning with Danny when he's got an idea in his head. And anything was better than just hanging round there all night.

So we all trouped off up the other end of Eppingham to Doug's house but of course he said he hadn't got any money either. He wouldn't even let us in. He said he'd got his cousins round and had to talk to them but it was more like he didn't want us finding his wallet and stealing his hoards.

'You tight bastard,' Mikey shouted into the doorway, so if there were any cousins they'd all hear.

Doug went bright red. 'Look, you'll have to go,' he said and pulled the door shut, leaving us standing there on his doorstep.

'Wanker,' Danny muttered.

We sat on Doug's front wall for a bit, pulling the leaves off his dad's rose bushes but then a nosey old guy came out from next door and made such a big thing of putting his bins out and hanging around watching us that we shuffled off again and started wandering back down towards the main road. I guess we were headed back to the petrol station. There was nowhere else to go. Mikey was mucking around, pushing Danny and Richard into the road so then they'd push him back. Then they started throwing sticks and kicking stones at passing cars as we walked by. It made me nervous, not because I thought my mum and dad might be in one of those cars. They never went out anywhere in the evenings, never ever. But there was always the chance it might be a neighbour or someone they knew, someone who'd tell on me. Not that we were doing anything wrong. But even so, it was better to be somewhere in a dark corner in Eppingham, instead of in the glare of the lights.

But it's a long road that stretches from one end of Eppingham to the other, and there's the motorway bridge right in the middle of it. No more houses on the motorway bridge, no more gardens, no sticks to pull. Just the wind, driving into our eyes, and the dull roar of the cars from below.

At the top of the bridge Mikey stopped and put his hands on the rail and leaned over and yelled, '*I'm bored!*' again, at the top of his voice.

'Shut the fuck up about being bored, will you?' Danny said.

'Well let's *do* something,' Mikey said. He let go of the rail and started jostling Danny, pushing at him, trying to get a response. 'Make me laugh. Entertain me.'

'Fuck off,' Danny said.

'Let me make you laugh then,' Mikey said and he put his hands back on the rail, and then he pulled one foot up and got that on the rail too. He turned his head to look at us and he was grinning, with this dare me look in his eyes. And then, so carefully, with all his weight on his arms, he pushed himself up, drawing up his other foot so he was perched on the rail and clinging on with his hands and feet like a monkey.

And probably we did laugh at first, at Mikey clinging to that rail like a monkey. And Mikey was laughing too, that staccato crack, firing off in the air. It didn't seem dangerous, not at first. He moved so carefully, so measured; his arms were strong. I thought if he fell he'd fall back onto the pavement where he'd started from but even so I said, 'Mikey, get down,' and I can hear myself now. *Oh, Mikey get down.* My girly voice, thin on the wind. And Danny calling him a tosser and Richard calling him a pratt but just me saying get down, and then saying it again and really meaning it because he started to uncurl, straightening his legs first and then letting go of the rail with his hands; his hands quavering in the air above the rail as he balanced there, bent over, and then slowly stood up.

'*For god's sake, Mikey, get down!*'

I have it seared behind my eyes: Mikey standing there on the rail with his back to us, his arms spread wide like Jesus Christ while the wind rippled his shirt and ripped at his hair. And then he turned to face us, lifting one foot and crossing it over the other as he twisted round but he missed his footing and rocked backwards and forwards and backwards again and his arms spun out like windmills; there was a flash of the blue of his jeans and the white of his shirt through the gaps in the railings, and he was gone.

I screamed, and the scream went on and on.

Somewhere on the edge of my scream there was Richard, slamming his body into the railings, lunging at the air with his arms outstretched, catching nothing. There was Richard's face, jaw yanked down in cartoon horror, screaming over the edge, then screaming back at us, 'He's hit the *cars*. He's hit the fucking *cars*.'

And beside me Danny was making this noise like he was laughing but couldn't get any air, and he doubled over like he'd got a stomach ache, wrapping his arms across his body and digging in his hands. I grabbed hold of his arm.

'Oh my God! Oh my God! *Do* something!' I yelled. 'Call an ambulance or something!' I tried to get my phone out my bag but I couldn't open the zip. I had this feeling in my legs like my bones had gone. I slipped right down the length of Danny and I was sitting on the ground. I couldn't breathe. I thought I was going to be sick. Richard *was* sick. He turned away from the railing and it splashed on the pavement, white flecks dotting over my legs and my bag. I couldn't open my bag. I swallowed and swallowed, water filling in my mouth.

Richard puked again and I felt the warmth of it hit the back of my hand.

'Danny, your *phone*,' I said. 'Get your *phone*. Call an *ambulance*. Quick!' But Danny was backing away, just saying, 'Jesus oh Jesus,' over and over. You could hear the cars below; the screech of brakes, someone's hand on the horn, stuck. I couldn't look but I could see it in my head anyway, Mikey buffeting from car to car like a rag doll, Mikey breaking up.

'The *cars*,' Richard was saying and he kept looking and looking away. There was a string of dribble swinging from his chin.

I got out my phone. I was back on my feet now, sausage fingers jamming 999. I couldn't hear anyone answer, couldn't hear anything except the wind and the cars and my heartbeat ramming in my head. 'Ambulance,' I shouted anyway. 'Police.'

'Don't need the fucking police,' Danny shouted and he knocked my phone right out my hands.

'What are you *doing*?' I yelled and he yelled right back at me,

'What are *you* doing? You don't call the fucking police!'

'For God's sake, Danny, Mikey's fallen off the bridge!'

'I know he's fallen off the fucking bridge! I saw him fall off the fucking bridge!'

'We need the police!'

'We don't need the fucking police!'

He kicked my phone; he was going to kick it through the railings and down, the same way Mikey'd gone but I grabbed it back up and he kicked my hand instead. And we were standing there, having this row, and the police and the ambulance came anyway, sirens shrieking out below us.

'Oh Jesus,' Danny said and he grabbed hold of me, tried to drag me away but then there was a whirl of blue lights, sirens loud behind us, coming up on the bridge. 'Fuck!' Danny said and he let go of me and he *ran*, just leaving us there, me and Richard; he just ran and left us there.

The police put Richard and me in the back of their car, and they took us to Richard's house. I sat up close to Richard in the car, and on the sofa in his mum's front room. He held my hands, or did I hold his? And with his legs against mine I could feel this constant shiver, rippling its way through his body.

Richard's mum made us tea, which she brought in on a tray and put down on the coffee table, clucking her tongue and saying, 'Dear oh dear,' over and over. She'd put on the gas fire and the heat of it was like a blanket, though it didn't stop Richard from shivering. I needed the loo and she came with me, standing outside the door and saying, 'You all right in there, love?' every two seconds. I'd got jelly legs, numb all the way down. My feet prickled like needles every time I moved.

When I sat back down next to Richard he took hold of my hands again. His fingers were sticky, warm. The coals of the gas fire were roaring up blue, and intermittently bright orange streaks flared up and died down and flared up again. I followed the flames with my eyes, trying to see a pattern, trying to see anything other than Mikey, spread up there against the sky like Jesus.

'What were you doing up on that bridge?' the policeman asked and Richard just said, 'Walking.'

Did we not know it was a stupid thing to do, the policeman asked us, climbing up on the rails like that? Did we not know it was dangerous? But what could we say? He was asking the wrong person. Of course *we* knew it was stupid, of course *we* knew it was dangerous. But it wasn't us that had climbed up there, and was dead now. And he wanted to know who the other guy was, the one who'd run off, and I had to say it was Danny, it was my *boyfriend* and the word was thick on my tongue.

'Why did he run away?' the policeman asked but what could I say? 'Was he frightened? Do you think he might feel responsible?'

I shrugged my shoulders and shook my head at the same time and two tears plopped out and ran down my face and off my chin, triggering off a stream. I'd have wiped them away but Richard still had hold of my hands.

The policeman sighed. 'It isn't your fault,' he said but it may as well have been, for the way we felt, Richard and me, clinging hold of each others' hands.

Did Danny feel responsible?

Maybe he did, only I couldn't think that right then. Couldn't think how he was feeling, only that he'd run off, and left us like that.

I just wanted to stay sat on that sofa, numbed by the heat and the flicker of the gas fire but the policeman wanted to take me home. It was cold in the back of the car after Richard's living room, and without Richard beside me. I was going to be so late home. It's like, you want to just rewind time, close your eyes and just scratch it back and have the sick feeling in your stomach gone. You want to stop and go back and *stay* back and have it not happen. Forever and ever and ever, you want to shut your eyes and have it not happen.

All the lights were on at the house. They'd be waiting for me, worried or angry and if they'd tried to phone I hadn't heard it. Somehow this made it all worse, coming home in a police car, walking to my door with a policeman by my side. It made it so real. I could only think that Mikey wouldn't be going home, not tonight, not ever again. And that there'd have been a policeman knocking on his door, too, and telling his mum. His poor mum. And his poor dad, who worked at the insurance office in the High Street and you could see sitting at his desk when you walk by. And his poor nan, who gave him all the money that he spent on drugs.

My dad must have been looking out for me. The door opened before we reached it and there he was with this drawn-in look on his face and my mum pushing up behind him all flushed and ... *angry*. That's how she looked: angry. That I was late, that it was a *policeman* bringing me home, that it was a police car parked up outside our house; the shock, the horror, the shame of it. Automatically there's the assumption that I'm in trouble, that I've done something wrong. I could see it on her face. On both their faces. And there was me thinking – stupidly – that they'd see the police car and just be glad that I was OK. I'd had this daft idea that we were another family for a moment, the kind of family that pulls together when something bad happens, you know, *supporting* each other.

Not so.

They fairly yanked me inside. The policeman came in too, and my mum tried to push the door shut as far as she could with him standing there on the mat. Like she was trying to hide him from the neighbours, though they'd all have seen that car.

I stood in the hall on weak legs while the policeman told them what had happened. I was crying and all I wanted was for someone to put their arms around me and hold me, but no way. As soon as the policeman had gone they rounded on me.

'What's been going on?' my mum demanded like the policeman hadn't just told her. 'What have you been doing this time?'

I hadn't been *doing* anything. And what did she mean by *this time*? I stared at her, too numb to speak.

'Who *are* these boys you've been hanging around with?' she asked, making it sound like I was the village whore. 'Well? Who are they? Who is this Micky?'

'Mikey,' I whispered and the tears just kept on coming.

'Micky. Mikey. I've never even heard of the boy,' she huffed in her don't-pick-hairs-with-me tone. I couldn't believe her. Couldn't believe she was actually my mother. Mikey was dead, for God's sake. Didn't she *care*?

I looked at my dad; I wanted him to say something, just *something* to show that he had some idea of how I felt but he just looked back at me with this grey, disappointed expression on his face and said, 'It's late. I think we might all feel better after some sleep,' which was just the stupidest thing to say. How on earth was sleep going to make things any better?

I couldn't put the light off. Not that night, not for many nights.

I lay on my bed, curled on my side with my arms wrapped tight around me, hands jammed into my armpits. The shivers that had been going through Richard were going through me now. Every time I closed my eyes my stomach lurched and my body jolted, like when you think you're going to fall. Think of Mikey, think of him feeling like that only it going on and on . . . Try to think how many seconds there were, between that rail and the road below. I wanted to think and I didn't want to think. I stared at my light so hard that the glow of it had me blind, so I closed my eyes for a second but straight away my stomach turned over again and the shivers rolled. I could see Mikey, laughing at the top. And now I could see him on the way down, arms and legs flailing about in the air like an insect's, climbing on nothing.

* * *

It was Saturday the next day; I'd got the whole weekend stuck at home, with my parents.

'Don't you think you're going out,' my mum said to me when I eventually came downstairs in the morning. She kind of swooped across the kitchen to guard the back door, flinging out her arms so that a stash of scrunched-up tissues shot out of the filthy sleeves of her dressing-gown like ping-pong balls. What did she think I was going to do? Make a sudden run for it? Like, *why*? I was still in my nightie, for God's sake. And my legs were so wobbly they wouldn't have taken me anywhere.

'No, you needn't think you're going anywhere, young lady,' she went on, wagging at me now with her finger. 'You're not so much as stepping outside this house. Not until I've had some answers.'

Answers? What answers? I deliberately didn't look at her. I looked out of the window just beside her instead, and there was my dad, raking the leaves up off the lawn. Obviously he wasn't in too much of a hurry for answers.

'Mikey was a friend of Danny's,' I said, keeping my voice as flat as I could. 'We'd gone for a walk. He climbed onto the rail of the motorway bridge for a laugh, and he fell off. What else do you want me to say?'

It didn't matter what else. She'd heard all she needed

to hear in my first sentence. Mikey was *Danny's* friend.

'I might have known it would come back down to *him*,' she snapped.

For the rest of the weekend I lay around like I was ill, because I couldn't think what else to do with myself. *They* acted like this was all somehow my fault. My mum pretty well said as much.

'Your behaviour lately leaves an awful lot to be desired,' she stated and when that got no response she slammed down the washing basket she was carrying and got all hysterical. 'You're out of control!' she screamed, knickers and socks and tea towels falling all over the floor. I stayed where I was, on the sofa, ignoring her. 'Don't think you're going out!' she yelled, though I hadn't moved. 'Do you hear me?'

How could I not hear her? Though she could have saved herself the screeching. I didn't *want* to go out. The thought of ever having to go out again, and walk along that road that we'd walked along on Friday night, was freaking me out.

And anyway, the only reason I'd have gone out was to see Danny. But I hadn't even heard from Danny since he'd run off and left me and Richard on the bridge. Not a phone call, not even a text message. Somewhere, stuck back behind the horror of it all there was this little piece of hardened-up hurt. I knew, without a doubt, that he'd be expecting me to contact him. This was just so like Danny, to disappear, to create his own drama on top of everything else. I'd have played along, before.

But Friday night had put a line through things. There was before, and there was after. Before, I'd have phoned him.

But this was after.

And I wasn't the one who'd run away.

I so didn't want to go to school on Monday. Didn't see how I *could* go to school but my mum was there at seven-thirty, dragging me out of bed. And with such relish. She couldn't get me out the door fast enough.

'And you'd better go straight there,' she called up the street after me. 'I'll be phoning the school! I'll be checking on you!'

I didn't think for a minute that I'd see Danny. I mean, I really didn't *think* about him. I just thought about that bridge, and walking over it. And that I was walking over it on my own, and I didn't know if I could do it, though I did, of course, legs plodding on like lead. God, I would have liked anybody to walk with.

It was just so unreal. So like nothing had happened; there was the railing where he'd stood, there were the cars, just passing by, oblivious. I thought I'd home in on the exact spot but I wasn't so sure now. It could almost have not happened at all, if it wasn't for the image of Mikey stuck in my head, arms stretched wide to the sky.

Everyone was talking about it at school. I could hear them all, in the playground, the corridors, the classrooms . . . *Oh my God, did you hear about Mikey Petes?* Even people in my year, in my form group. People who didn't even know him, and who wouldn't have cared about him anyway, if they had. I could see them, racking their brains trying to think what Mikey looked like. But they couldn't come up with anything, so they looked at me instead. Death by association.

At lunchtime I hid in the loos. I locked myself in a cubicle and pulled the lid down and sat there with my feet drawn up so no one would see me from underneath. I'd got a pain in my head that had been there all weekend and was getting worse and I didn't think it would ever go away. I closed my eyes and felt my eyeballs tighten into themselves till I could see the purple inside my head. I wanted to be invisible. I wanted to disappear into a blank sleep and sleep forever.

I dropped my head onto my knees. Vaguely I heard the bell for the end of lunch but I ignored it. I stayed locked in that loo till gone half past three when everyone else had gone home and the cleaner came slamming in with her bucket, and thumped on the door.

* * *

Danny was sitting on someone's wall at the end of the school road. He watched me walking towards him. No smile of course. Smiles were all finished with, now.

'Where have you been?' he snapped so I snapped straight back,

'Nowhere.'

'You're late,' he said, as if I should have known he was waiting for me.

'Well you weren't there this morning,' I said. 'And how do you think I felt, walking over that bridge on my own? And then at school, having everyone talking about it?' My voice caught; he heard it and lowered his head.

'I couldn't face it,' he mumbled.

'Do you think I could?' I said. 'I had no choice.' I was still standing. I looked down at him, at the stoop of his shoulders and the top of his head; at his hair, grown long and curling off the collar of his jacket. There were so many different feelings crashing through my heart that I couldn't have picked out any one from the other.

'You didn't call me,' he said. He was picking at the edge of his thumb nail, digging a tear into the skin.

'*You* didn't call *me*,' I said. 'And it was you that ran off.'

'You should have come with me, Louise,' he said. His thumb was bleeding. Slowly he smeared the blood across his nail. 'I wanted you to come with me.'

'I *had* to stay. *You* should have stayed.'

'You *chose* to stay,' he said. 'With Richard.'

He was twisting things. He always twisted things. I could feel myself pulled every way. 'I didn't choose to stay with Richard,' I said. 'It wasn't like that.'

'And you went back to his house.' He looked at me now, eyes narrowed, like he'd got me cornered. 'He told me everything.'

There was nothing *to* tell. Not the way he meant it. But even so I felt myself needing to explain, to *justify*. 'The police took us there,' I said. 'Before they took me home. God it was awful, Danny. And you weren't there.'

'I needed you, Louise,' he said and he dropped his head again, into his hands. 'I needed you so much.'

I could feel tears, stinging in my eyes and the ache in my head was getting worse. We shouldn't be arguing. Not now. This . . . all this . . . it was too big. I sat down beside him and leant my head against his shoulder. I could feel the rise and fall of his body as he sighed, and sighed again.

'I can't stop thinking about it, Louise,' Danny said. 'It's doing my head in. I need you. I need you with me.'

He turned and he held me and I held him back. We were both crying. Hadn't I just so, so wanted to be held, since Friday night? No one else held me. No one else cared. So we sat there on that wall, glued together like that for I don't know how long while the cars and the buses went by and someone blasted their horn and the daylight began to dip.

He walked me home. There was just this numbness, walking back up the bridge, in me, in him too, I think. Someone had sellotaped a bunch of flowers to the railing since this morning; limp little blue things that looked like they'd been rotting in a bucket outside a petrol station for ages. I can't tell you how pathetic they looked, and how much I didn't want to see them.

Danny didn't want to see them either. He kicked the heads off them as we walked past.

'Stupid fucking bastard's put them in the wrong place,' he said. 'It wasn't there. It wasn't there he jumped, was it, Louise? It was here.' He put his hand on this one exact spot on the railings, just centimetres from where those flowers were. And he moved his fingers over the metal, really gently, barely touching it at all, as if he was tracing Mikey's footprint. 'It was right here.' He was staring so intently, at the railing, and then at the sky, as if Mikey's image had left its mark up there, too. And then he looked over, down at the cars, zooming under the bridge, oblivious. I couldn't do that. I couldn't look down.

'Right here,' he said again, so certain.

* * *

'You're late again,' my mum snapped the minute I got in. 'Do I have to start coming out to meet you? Do I? Do I?'

What was she shouting for? Did she think I couldn't hear her? I walked out the kitchen and through the hall, to go upstairs. She followed, breathing fast, shallow, working herself up into a fit.

'Do I?' she yelled again, right close to my ear, and I ran up the stairs, away from her.

'It's that boy!' she shouted after me. 'Don't think I don't know it! You've been with that boy when you should have been coming home!'

I slammed my bedroom door shut behind me, hard. Didn't she stop for a second to think how *that boy* might be feeling right now? Didn't she stop to think how *I* might be feeling? Did she *ever* stop to think about anything outside her own miserable little world?

On the day of Mikey's funeral I bunked off school and Danny and I went down to the boathouse and smoked cigarette after cigarette. It was biting cold; raw, damp cold cutting into us all day. It seemed fitting somehow. Seemed fitting that we should have to be cold when they stuck Mikey into the ground.

We should have gone to the funeral. Often I think that. We should have gone, but we were too scared.

* * *

That night we went round Richard's. It was the first time I'd seen him since it had happened. He'd been to the funeral. Out of all of us, he was the only one.

We were squashed up in his bedroom, all three of us sat on his bed. We'd taken up mugs of tea and Richard was clutching on to his with shaking hands. His cup was too full and tea splashed across his knuckles. He was so pale that under the shadow of his hair his skin looked blue.

'Why weren't you there?' he said to Danny. 'Mikey was your mate too.'

Danny just shrugged but I felt really bad. He should have gone. And I should have done too, but how could I without Danny? That would have really pissed him off.

'Couldn't face it,' Danny said. 'Can't stand funerals.'

Richard sipped at his tea and pulled this kind of *who can?* face. Danny didn't see it, but I did. And stupidly I said, 'What was it like?'

'Fucking awful,' Richard said. 'Mikey's mum didn't stop crying the whole time.'

Tears were pricking at my own eyes just thinking about it. But it didn't seem right to cry now; I should have gone to the funeral for that.

'Was Bez there?' Danny asked.

'No,' Richard said, and Danny nodded as if that

made things right. As if it was OK that he hadn't gone, seeing as Bez hadn't either. Solidarity and all that. Some people deal with things *differently*. And then he said, 'I think he planned it.'

We both looked at him. '*What?*' Richard said.

'I think he planned to jump.'

'No he didn't,' Richard said.

'I think he did.' Danny leant forward, convinced with his own theory. 'I think . . .' he said, pausing for emphasis '. . . it was suicide.'

'It wasn't fucking suicide,' Richard said.

And I said, 'Danny, he fell. He was just mucking around.'

'Maybe he was depressed,' Danny said.

'Mikey wasn't depressed.' Richard was tapping his middle finger against his cup, fast, in agitation. 'And he was laughing when he climbed up. You don't *laugh* if you're about to commit fucking suicide.'

'Yeah, but maybe that was all just a front. A decoy. Maybe he'd got it planned all along. Depressed people sometimes hide what they're feeling, don't they? Maybe *he* hid it.'

'He wasn't depressed, all right, he was just fucking stupid,' Richard said, and in a flash Danny leapt right across me and smashed the cup right out of his hands, and they both went crashing off the bed and onto the floor, taking everything off the top of Richard's bedside table with them.

I screamed, before I could stop myself.

'Don't you call him fucking stupid,' Danny spat into Richard's face. He'd got his fist in Richard's face and he would have thumped the hell out of him only Richard was just as strong; he'd got his arms out rigid, hands digging into Danny's shoulders, holding him off.

'Danny, stop it!' I yanked at his T-shirt, trying to pull him back. I couldn't see his face, only Richard's – the sweat beading above his eyes, the teeth clenched.

A door banged downstairs, and Richard's mum was shouting up, 'Richard! What's going on up there? What's all that banging around?'

'Nothing, Mum,' Richard managed to shout back, and he pushed Danny off. 'I just knocked my lamp over.'

'That was a lot of noise for a lamp,' she yelled back.

'It's OK, Mrs Wellan,' I called in my nicest voice. 'It isn't broken.'

Danny wasn't saying anything. He was staring at Richard like he was going to go for him again. Richard was staring back at him with something like disbelief on his face. 'You want to just back off,' he said. 'Just fucking back off.'

It was front page in the local paper. *Local boy in suicide fall*. My mum left it out for me to see. There was a picture of him in his school clothes, tie done up neat, hair combed. I don't think I'd ever seen Mikey looking like that.

'Look,' she gloated, jabbing Mikey's face with her finger. 'It says here he was just fourteen years old. Shocking it is, shocking . . .' She slapped her tongue against the roof of her mouth in an exaggerated tut. 'I blame the parents,' she said, and turned over to the letters page.

Whenever I saw Danny in the days that followed I'd automatically check out his face, to try and gage his mood.

Tonight it wasn't good.

He'd been round Mikey's, earlier, to see Mikey's mum.

And he couldn't understand why she wasn't pleased to see him.

'She didn't even let me in,' he said. 'Just stood in that fucking doorway with the door open this much – just this much –' he held his hands up, barely centimetres apart '– and couldn't wait to slam it back again in my face.'

What could I say? I could only think of poor Mikey's mum, and how she must feel.

'Bitch,' Danny said, walking on, fast. He'd got hold of my hand, tight. I didn't know where we were going. The boathouse maybe, maybe not. Sometimes when he was like this it was best to be going nowhere, but just to keep walking. 'I bet she'd have been a lot nicer if it'd been Bez knocking on her door.'

'I doubt it,' I said.

'She wouldn't have shut the door in Bez's face,' he said, as if I hadn't spoken.

'Oh come off it, Danny,' I said, because I couldn't believe he thought that, not really. 'What on earth do you think she'd want to see Bez for? Unless it *was* just to slam the door in his face.'

'Bez was Mikey's mate.' He stopped walking. I should have heeded the warning, but all I wanted was for him to wake up, see sense.

'Some mate.'

'What do you mean by that?'

'Who was it that Mikey got his dope off? Who was it had him stoned all the time?' I said *who was it Mikey got his dope off*, but I meant *you too* and he knew it. He'd still got hold of my hand, and he shook it, hard, just once, so the jolt of it bolted all the way up, right into my shoulder.

'Shut up,' he said. 'Mikey wasn't stoned all the time. He wasn't stoned that night.'

'No, but he was bored. He was *bored* because he *wasn't* stoned.'

'Shut up,' Danny said again. There was a bright light in his eyes. Anger like I ought to have been scared out of my head, but I'd had enough.

'No I won't shut up.' My heart was kicking against my chest but I ignored it. 'Mikey, Richard, you – you're all only happy when you're stoned. Don't you realise how *boring* that is? And you think Bez is your friend? He sounds like a dickhead if you ask me.'

'Well I didn't ask you,' Danny said and he grabbed me with both hands; I thought he was going to hit me but he just shook me, hard, and pushed me away. I toppled backwards, nearly ending up on my backside and he just turned and stormed off, away down the street.

I didn't go after him and he didn't look back.

Well, good. I was angry too. I was angry every bit as much as he was.

But the next day there were a hundred messages on my phone. *Come round. We need to talk. I need you. I'm sorry.*

He was babysitting Ellie. When I got there he didn't want to talk, he wanted to make love to me and I guess that's all I wanted too because there were no words between Danny and me any more except the same

197

words, the same old words, saying nothing, going nowhere.

Ellie was stuck in front of the TV, threatened with death if she so much as put a foot on the stairs. We went up to his room and the second he closed the door he was holding me, clinging to me hard, wrapping his body right up tight with mine like he could never get close enough. Like he was trying to drive a way out of himself. And afterwards he just held on to me, with his face pressed against my neck, saying, 'Don't ever leave me,' over and over again, whispered into my skin. I could feel his breath, so warm, so *close*. 'Don't leave me. I couldn't stand it. First my dad, then Mikey. I couldn't bear to lose you too.'

And I blocked out my ears to the voice in my head telling me it was over. How could it ever be over? What choice did I have?

There was just too much between us now. Too much for either of us to ever really be free.

12

My parents got a call from the school. I'd bunked off
once – just once, on the day Mikey was buried – and
someone was on the phone, checking up on me. I just
can't believe it. Other people – Danny, for example –
bunked off all the time but did this happen to them? I
don't think so. But then they weren't *promising* like me,
so I guess they weren't worth chasing up.

It makes me sick just to think about it.

My parents went ballistic. I mean *one day* was all I'd
missed. One lousy day, and for what reason? I was hardly
having fun, for God's sake, but they didn't stop to think
about that. They didn't stop to think about anything but
their own bad ideas about me.

'What were you doing?' yelled my mum. '*Trawling the
streets?*'

Even my dad was angry. In fact it was only the
third time I'd ever seen him angry in my life, the first
being years ago when Natalie and I cut all the flowers
off his rose bush to make rose water, the second being
the time my mum threw that cup at him, and he walked
out. He wasn't even that angry over the smoking

incident. Not really. He'd much rather have avoided it all.

But this was different. A call from the school. My, my, they'd have beaten me, they'd have locked me up if they could. I think this was the first time in my life I'd ever seen them united in anything.

'It's that boy again!'

'What kind of a reputation do you think you're getting yourself?'

'Hanging around on street corners!' (Oh come *on*.) 'Getting into trouble!'

'Yes, you'll be getting into *trouble*! Boys like that! Don't think I don't know!'

'Smoking! Drinking! Whatever next!'

I am making half of this up. Truth is I can't remember what they said just that they ranted and raved and called me every kind of disgrace under the sun while I stood there trying to shut out my ears. They fired each other off. My mum would shriek one thing and my dad would agree, add a bit to it, and then she'd hurl out something else. He was giving her free reign for the first time in her life, no limit to the hysterics, no *Calm down, calm down*.

Look what a favour I'd done their marriage. You'd think they'd be grateful. Why, I'd brought them together at last.

Funny how you can detach yourself when you need to.

Eventually I was allowed to escape and go to my room. No, sorry, I was *sent* to my room. No supper that night. It would seem the traditional punishments are best, in our house.

Traditional punishment gets a traditional response. So I lay on my bed, crying. Not because I'd been told off, or I was ashamed, God no, though that's what they'd like to think. I was crying because I was wondering how much more shit a person could take, and because every now and then it just got to me, how much my mother seemed to hate me.

My mum's got a drawer full of my baby things. Little knitted booties, bonnets and christening bracelets, things like that. There's a Peter Rabbit cup and a shawl my granny knitted, and a tiny little tin with what must be a lock of my horrible hair in it. Sometimes I sneak into her room and look at these things. I don't remember them. I don't recognise them as mine though they must be of course because there've been no other babies in this house. What gets me is that she keeps them all, tucked up in her drawer. There's a little white photo album too, with pictures of the lovely little me inside it, from way back in the good old days before I went and ruined it all by growing up.

When I ventured downstairs the next morning she was standing at the kitchen table, and she'd got that photo album out. As soon as I walked in she started turning the pages, roughly, licking her finger and snatching at the corners. The paper the pictures were stuck onto was old and delicate; I could hear it catching and ripping against her nail. And I could hear her, muttering and sighing and grinding her teeth.

I ignored her. I just wanted to grab my shoes and my jacket and be gone.

'Can you believe it? *Can* you believe it?' There was that shrill note in her voice, pitching up. 'What did I do to deserve this? Where did I go so wrong?'

She wanted a reaction but she wasn't going to get one from me. I'd got my stuff but she was blocking my way; I had to take my chance and bolt past her, back into the hall and out the front.

'Tell me!' she screeched at me. 'Where did I go so wrong?' She flung that photo album at me and it hit me square on the back of the head. I didn't stop; I yanked the front door open, I was out of there. 'Don't you go seeing that boy!' she yelled up the street after me. 'Do you hear me? And if he comes round here looking for you he'll get a piece of my mind.'

She needn't have got herself into such a state. I hardly ever saw Danny these days. He was too busy out getting stoned with Bez.

'Louise, could I have a word with you at break this morning, please?' Mrs Neil said at the end of registration, and then I just knew that she was the one who'd called up my parents.

I stared at her sitting there with her face totally unmoved, oblivious to the hell she'd caused for me. She couldn't care less, sitting there, ticking off names. She wasn't even looking at me.

I was in half a mind to just ignore her and not turn up at break but then I thought she'd probably go and phone my parents again. When I did get to the form room she wasn't even there, so what now? Did I wait, for this conversation that I didn't want to have, or what? I was about to go when casually she shuffled up, coffee cup in hand. Didn't think to get one for me.

'Ah Louise,' she said, looking at me now like she'd never really had a good look before. I saw her scanning my face for make-up, checking out my hair. Maybe she was looking for tips; she could certainly do with a few.

She sat herself down and sipped at her coffee, both hands clasped around the cup with the sleeves of her hideous long cardi pulled down over her knuckles like she was cold.

'I understand you're planning to go to Meadlands,' she said, putting that cup down on the desk with her hands still wrapped round it. 'I had a little chat with your mother yesterday.' She paused, staring at me, like she expected me to say something. Did she think I'd be surprised? Did she think I didn't *know* about her little chat with my mother?

'Well if you want to go to Meadlands you need to work very, very hard. You'll need high grades in all your GCSEs. You can do it, Louise. You can if you try but you're not trying. You've become . . . distracted. You know what I'm talking about, Louise, don't you? Don't you?'

I tried not to listen to what she was saying. I had to. I'd die rather than cry in front of *her*. I concentrated on her cardigan for distraction, counting the snagged-out knobbles in the wool. How old could such a gross cardigan be?

Mrs Neil sighed. 'We're worried about you,' she said, going for the soft approach now. 'All of us. Your parents. Your teachers. We want to see you do your best.'

I fixed my eyes on that puddle-grey wool. There was one long ladder, running right out from under her arm.

'I know things have been ... difficult for you recently,' she said. 'Do you want to talk to me about it?'

I shook my head, fast, and that was the worst thing; these tears came out of nowhere, running down. I wanted to die. I wanted to get out of there.

'Take your time,' she said, kindly, too kindly. 'I'm here if you need me.'

I couldn't get out of there fast enough. I didn't even care who saw me, running down the corridor with tears streaming down my face. What difference did it make to me what people saw or thought or said about me? I was beyond that, way beyond, I was stretched out as far as I could go.

I slammed into the loos and locked myself in a cubicle and sat on the stinking seat with my head in my hands and cried and cried like I might get some relief out of it but I didn't. Crying made it worse. Crying just gave me hot eyes and a headache and this awful, empty feeling inside.

That afternoon I came out of school late, deliberately. I'd avoided everyone all day and I wanted to carry on avoiding them. But then just up ahead I saw Cara, on her own, and suddenly I so, so wished things were how they used to be. I didn't know what I was doing, I didn't think, I just ran up beside her, and caught her up.

She looked at me like I needn't have bothered.

'I'm sorry,' I blurted out because I couldn't think what else to say and straight away I was crying again, like there was this tap in my head, unstoppable. Her stony face eased up, just a little and she put her arm around me.

'I didn't mean things to be like this,' I said, with the tears dripping off my chin. 'I am so sorry.'

'Are you still going out with Danny?' Cara asked, like that was the crucial thing. The make or break: was I still going out with *Danny Fisher*?

'I don't know,' I said. 'Kind of.'

'Well ditch him,' she said. 'You've got to. I mean, it's not like he's making you happy, is it?'

I wished things were that simple. I really, really did. 'I don't know,' I said. 'It's complicated. Mikey . . .'

I sounded pathetic even to my own ears. Cara dropped her hand and looked away, cold again.

I hardly ever saw Danny but I got endless text messages. It was like a running commentary going over what had happened that night, with Mikey.

He didn't scream when he fell, what does that mean?

It was suicide, he was driven to it by that bitch of a mother.

Did you see Richard push him?

None of it made any sense. Then there was all this

stuff about us getting away, any day now, me and him, soon. The same old dream, not given up.

I knew it was just words, mixed up words. But all I heard when I read message after weird message was how much Danny needed me.

13

Danny got a Ouija board from somewhere. He said that was the only way to really find out if Mikey meant to fall or not.

'We'll ask him,' he said, like that it was that simple, and he dragged me by the hand up to Richard's house and from there we all went on to Doug's. 'You've got to have four people,' Danny said. 'Three's not enough.'

He was striding ahead, pulling me with him, with Richard skulking along way behind. Richard didn't want to do it; that was obvious. I didn't want to do it. But if Danny was going to start playing around with a Ouija board I had to be there. God knows what might happen. Maybe I could hold him back if things went too far. Maybe.

It was a stupid, dangerous thing to do.

'We'll take it to the graveyard,' Danny said. 'That's the best place.'

'Don't be daft, Danny. We might get caught.'

'So what? There's no law against it.'

'It won't work outside. It's too windy, it's too . . .'

But there was no point in trying to put him off. He

was driven, from deep inside. It was like he thought he'd be chatting to Mikey again, one to one.

But then Doug couldn't come out because his parents were out and he had to look after his brother. So now it was a choice of graveyard and no Doug, or all four of us, here.

We ended up setting the board out on Doug's bedroom floor with one of Doug's mum's crystal glasses from downstairs, stuck in the middle. And then we sat around, in a circle, and looked at it.

'Turn out the light,' Danny said, and he started rolling up a spliff.

'You can't smoke in here, mate,' Doug said. 'My parents will kill me if they smell it.'

But Danny lit up anyway, and Doug jumped up and opened up the window and stood there frantically trying to chase the smoke out with one of his dodgy magazines. I took the joint off Danny just for one quick toke; I needed it to calm my nerves. It was dead creepy in there already, especially now we were in the dark. And we hadn't even begun yet.

'What now then?' Richard said.

'You've got to get up the right atmosphere,' Danny said and he was doing that all right, all by himself, with his voice slow and hushed, and his eyes blackened out in the dark and staring at each of us in turn.

'Danny, it's too dark in here. We can't even see the board,' I said.

'I can see.' He took a last long draw on that joint, then nipped out the burn with his fingers. Vaguely he looked round for somewhere to put it and he was going to just flick it away in a corner but in a flash Doug was there, back on his feet, snatching it up and headed for the window.

'For God's sake sit down,' Danny snapped and he did. This was it. 'Put your hand on the glass. Your left hand.'

Why your left hand? I wanted to ask but I didn't. No one was saying a thing. We'd all got our arms stuck out, one finger on that glass, like all we could do was obey orders. Suddenly I wanted to laugh. I kind of giggled, and I looked around, wanting someone else to join in, Richard maybe; he didn't want to be doing this any more than I did.

'Shut up,' Danny barked at me and in that second the glass was moving, taking all of us with it; it slammed out across the board to the letter N.

'Jesus,' Richard said.

'You pushed it,' Doug said, staring at Danny, then at me. 'It was him, he pushed it.'

Instantly the glass shot back the other way, straight to the letter A.

'NA. NA. What does it mean?' Danny was saying. 'Mikey, Mikey are you there?'

'It's you, it's you,' Doug squawked, getting himself half hysterical now, trying to get his hand off the glass but he couldn't. He was wriggling it and pulling at it but it was stuck, fast.

'Fuck off, Doug,' Richard hissed under hiss breath.

'Mikey,' Danny said, almost shouting. 'Can you hear me?' The glass shot across the board again, so fast it was lifting, tilting up on one side. It stopped, sharp, on the T.

'What are you trying to tell us?' Danny called. 'NAT? What does it mean?'

I knew what it meant. There was panic like nothing on earth gripping me tight across my shoulders. There was a scream in my chest but I couldn't swallow, couldn't hardly breathe. The tip of my finger was burning against the glass, I didn't want to see what we were spelling out. I knew it already. We'd got another A, an L; I knew the rest, didn't need to see it.

Doug had left the window open; suddenly it flipped on its hinges, slammed shut and the scream burst out. The glass toppled and I yanked free my hand.

'What the fuck are you doing?' Danny hissed at me. 'You've broken the circle.'

But I didn't care. I was out of there, so out of there.

212

I got out of that room, down the stairs and out of Doug's house and I swear I could feel Natalie, right there, with me. Natalie, who I'd longed and longed to have back again and now that she was I was freaking right out of my head.

I ran, out of Doug's road and down the next. I didn't stop till I was on the High Street with the bright lights from the shops and the street lights and the cars zooming by. I still felt like Natalie was behind me. And Mikey too for all I knew. It was *stupid*, trying to call up ghosts. *Stupid*. I heard footsteps coming up behind and I walked faster, too out of breath to run again, too out of breath to scream. I could feel my legs starting to crumble, then this hand on my arm—

'Louise.' It was Richard. 'Louise, stop. Are you OK?'

I was crying so hard now, with my eyes squeezed shut, blind. He put his arm around me, pulling me against his chest, just holding me. I don't know what I was crying for most – for Natalie, for Mikey, or just for myself, caught up in all this mess.

'What are you doing here?' I said, as soon as I could say anything and Richard's hold on me loosened.

'Danny wants you to come back,' he said.

'Well I'm not. I can't. No way.'

Richard stroked his hand back and forth across my shoulder, carefully, like I was something he didn't ought to touch. I could feel him weighing things up.

I could feel the shackles Danny had put on me, weighing me down.

'He sent me out to get you,' Richard said.

'Why couldn't he come himself?' I said, and I was crying again, choking out the words. 'I'm not going back. No way. It's stupid, trying to call up spirits. What good can it do? It's just stupid, the whole thing.'

Richard sighed. I could feel him, battling with himself. 'Come on,' he said at last, 'I'll walk you home.'

We didn't say anything else, the whole way back to my house. It would have felt disloyal, somehow, to speak. That was the kind of hold Danny had over us.

But when we got to my house he kissed me once, on the cheek.

'Take care,' he whispered, with something like sadness in his voice.

I wanted out.

I lay on my bed in the dark with my eyes wide open, whispering the words. *Danny, it's over, I'm sorry. It's over. It's over.*

My heart was speeding up as I mouthed the words and there was this feeling on my skin that was always there these days, like fear, like something round the corner.

It's over.

I could say it in the dark. I could say it when he couldn't hear.

He was waiting for me when I came out of school the next day. He was in a foul mood; no smiles, no hello. Not even a word till we were away from the gates and headed down towards the river. At least I guessed that was where we were going; he'd got me by the hand, walking fast and I trotted along beside him like I had no other choice.

It's over. It's over.

I could feel my heart, dragging inside.

There's a field that leads down to the river, covered in dog shit and churned up into mud in the rain; we squelched our way across. My feet were getting wet inside my shoes and I had to grip on tight to his hand to stop myself slipping.

There were some benches on the other side of the field, through the trees. We sat down, he lit us both us a cigarette, and I waited.

'I never thought you'd do this to me,' he said, so quietly, slumped down on that bench and gazing at the river.

I stared at him; at the side of his face as he drew on his cigarette. 'Do what?'

'Go off with my so-called mates behind my back.'

'What do you mean?' I said, and he snapped round, staring at me now, eyes firing up.

'Last night. You and Richard. You're fucking traitors, both of you.'

'Danny, I just wanted to get away from that Ouija board.'

'So you fucking ran off with Richard.'

'I did not. He came after me. He said you sent him.'

'I sent him to bring you back. Not to get off with you.'

'He did not get off with me. He walked me home.'

'You know he wants to fuck you.'

'Oh for God's sake.' I stood up to go and he stuck a hand out, pulling me back down.

'What am I supposed to think when you go off behind my back?'

'I did not go off behind your back.'

'I've seen the way he looks at you. The way he creeps around you.' He'd got both his hands on my arms now, fingers digging in through my sleeves.

'I can't believe I'm hearing this,' I said, and I tried to pull away.

'And you, leading him on,' he said, and something inside me snapped.

'It's over.' The words came out on their own. I

couldn't believe I'd said them. He stopped rock still, fingers pinching into my arms. 'Danny, it's over,' I said again and inside me I felt something lift. Just for a moment, I felt free.

But then he had me yanked up against him, hard, and he started kissing me and pressing his body against mine. 'Don't you ever fucking tell me it's over,' he said, the words hot and tight on my face. 'It's not over. It's never over.' He was crying, I could feel his tears on my face, taste them in my mouth. 'I love you, Louise. I'll fucking die if I haven't got you. I love you. Don't you ever try and tell me that it's over.'

He walked me back, to the corner. *Don't tell me it's over*, he said but I saw the darkness in his eyes when he said goodbye. You go so far. You go so far and no matter what you want, you can't turn back.

But I knew he wouldn't give up. He still met me in the mornings, and sometimes after school, too. And he sent me text after text, telling me how much he loved me.

I knew it was ownership. I knew it was a case of if he couldn't have me then nor could anyone else. And I knew it would make no difference in the end.

But if I look deep inside myself I also know that there was some dark part of me that didn't want him to give up. There was this little part of me that couldn't let go. I was hooked on the drama, on being loved like that. You can't just give it up, love like that.

And then one rotten, freezing wet day in December the school boiler packed up. Danny had met me at the top of his road and walked to school with me, but when we got there it was shut and there was this big sign on the gates sending everyone home.

A few people were milling around, staring at the sign like they couldn't understand it, even though Mr Walker was the other side of the gates in an oversized black plastic mac, yelling at them to go home while the rain ran off his hood and onto his nose.

'What's the matter with you all? Can't you read?' he kept shouting, waving his arms about in the air like he was chasing chickens. A couple of boys were lobbing stones or something at the gates but it was so wet and cold that most people really were just turning straight round and going home.

We started walking back the way we'd come. We couldn't talk because it was just too cold, and too much effort trying to keep the sleet out of our faces. I'd got my umbrella up but it was collapsed down at one side and I had to hold it low down over my head for it to do any good, and the backs of my hands and my knuckles were so cold they hurt. Danny kept alternating between ducking under the umbrella with me, and ducking out again. Either way he was risking getting a spoke in the eye.

We'd got as far as the bridge when Danny said, 'Come back to mine?'

He said it so easily, and so easily I could just have said yes. Often I think how I could have said yes. But I knew what would happen if I did go back to his house, and that then we'd just carry on like before and I didn't want that. He'd think everything was fine again and it wouldn't be. It *couldn't* be.

So I hesitated, and something flickered behind his charm. 'Or maybe you have other plans,' he said and something in his voice sent a warning prickling up my spine. But how could I possibly have had time to make any other plans? And so what if I had?

We carried on walking, and I was on my own under the umbrella now, but then I noticed something that now I think maybe Danny had noticed already: Richard was just a little way up ahead of us, walking on his own. He thought I didn't want to go back with him because of *Richard*. He thought that was why I hesitated. I can see that with hindsight. There's so much I can see, with hindsight.

Richard's house was just over the bridge and he

walked slowly; by the time we got to his house he was just putting his key in the door.

'Hello, Richard,' Danny said and there was that note in his voice again, some kind of *threat*.

Richard heard it too. Somewhat coolly he said hello back but that was it. He was going to close the door and leave us standing there but Danny grabbed hold of my hand and said, 'Well are you going to ask us in or not?' And Richard shrugged and we squeezed past him, dripping rain into the hall.

Danny's grip on my hand was tight and there were warning bells going off in the back of my head now. I tried not to hear them; I mean there was nothing unusual about us calling at Richard's. He was home, it was raining, we had all day to kill. I could hear myself, reeling off these normal, totally OK reasons in my head, but it wasn't OK. The tension in Danny's grip on my hand told me it wasn't OK.

We followed Richard into the living room. He sat on the chair, and we took the sofa but the second we'd sat down Danny made as if to get up again and said, all sarcastic, 'Oh sorry, Richard, did you want to sit here?'

I kind of laughed, out of embarrassment, I guess, but Richard just ignored him. He leaned forward, fiddling with the switch on the gas fire till it clicked into life and the coals lit up blue, turning the wet on our clothes and our hair into steam.

'Well isn't this nice?' Danny said with this sneer in his voice. He was sitting right forward on the sofa, elbows on his knees, fingers flicking and picking at his nails. It was an old sofa, squashy, and I'd sat back into it and was stuck there, sunk down. There was a little pulse of nerves, cramping in my stomach.

'Listen, mate, have you got something you want to say?' Richard said at last and Danny snapped right back,

'No, I think you've got something you want to say.' There was a nerve jamming away in his left leg, like a spasm, jigging it up and down. 'Haven't you, eh? Something you want to tell me about my girlfriend.'

'Danny, for God's sake,' I said and suddenly I felt way too vulnerable stuck back in those cushions and I tried to wriggle myself forward.

Danny's hand shot out and pushed me right back. 'Something you want to say about what you want to *do* to my girlfriend.' The hand that had pushed me was trailing up my arm now, across my collar bone, down, towards my chest. 'You want to do this.' The hand moved further. 'You want to touch her. Here.'

'Danny, get off,' I said but it was a red rag to a bull. He grabbed me, started kissing me, ramming his tongue

221

into my mouth. I couldn't breathe, couldn't think quick enough. This wasn't love. This was vile.

'Cut it out,' I heard Richard say, and Danny stopped, and slowly turned his face away from mine. He stared at Richard.

Richard stared back, his dark eyes inscrutable.

'What did you say?' Danny said.

'Just cut it out,' Richard said again. 'You're out of order.'

Danny laughed but it was a nasty laugh, glass-sharp and brittle. 'You're the one that's fucking out of order,' he said. 'Sniffing around my girlfriend all the time.' He went to grab me again but I pushed him off and he shoved me, hard, against the side of the sofa. My heart was banging against my ribs. *This* was why I wanted out. 'I mean, did you think I hadn't noticed? Did you think I hadn't noticed you sniff-sniff-sniffing around?'

Richard said nothing, just sat there staring at Danny, dark red colour creeping slowly into his face.

Danny took his cigarettes out his back pocket, stuck one in his mouth, and lit it. He didn't even offer me one, for the first time ever. Then he started ripping out the inside of the box and rolling it up, like he was making a roach, but he rolled it right up tight and flicked it at Richard. It hit him smack on the nose.

Richard blinked, nothing else, so Danny threw his

lighted cigarette at him; it caught in his hair, sizzled and dropped down beside him into the chair.

I screamed.

'Jesus!' Richard yelled, and jumped right out of that chair, and started digging around for that cigarette. He was bashing at the cushions with his hand; already you could smell the burning.

Danny sat back, and laughed, now he'd got a reaction. 'Wanker,' he said.

'*Danny*,' I said and he shot round at me, not laughing any more.

'Don't you fucking take his side,' he snapped.

'For God's sake, Danny.' There was this tightness in my head. I just couldn't deal with him when he was like this. He was staring at me, eyes dark, fired up. What was I meant to do? Fall into a heap? *What?*

'Just get out, will you?' Richard said.

'Don't worry. We're going,' Danny said, standing up, but I stayed put.

'I'm not going anywhere with you.'

Danny reached down, took hold of my arm. His nails were digging into my skin. '*Come on*,' he said.

I looked up at him. I could see all my own fears in his eyes, like there was this invisible chain between us. You can't break it. My God, you can't break it. My heart was thumping and weirdly there were the words of some

song going round in my head: *It ain't over till it's over* . . .
'No,' I said.

For seconds Danny's eyes were locked on mine and
he still had hold of my arm; already I was thinking, *What
am I doing?* And I was going to change my mind; I was
going to get up and go with him but then Richard said,
'You heard her. She's not going.'

Danny let go of my arm. And he started nodding his
head, like he'd got it right all along. 'Of course,' he said,
'you want to stay here with him.' And he spun away
from me and he grabbed Richard or thumped him or
something, or maybe it was Richard who thumped first,
I don't know. It doesn't matter. But suddenly they were
out in the hall and I'd no choice but to follow; Danny'd
got Richard up against the wall with his hand slamming
into his throat, calling him a wanker and a bastard. . . .
I was screaming at him to stop, screaming. Richard had
got his hand in Danny's face, forcing him off, and he
was pushing him towards the front door, just trying to
get him out.

I got the door open. And then we were outside,
Danny and me, out in the rain. He'd got a scratch
coming out of his top lip and into the skin under his
nose. It was rising up, purple on white, and he was
breathing hard, like he couldn't catch his breath.

'What is the matter with you?' I said but I didn't wait

for an answer, didn't want one. I started walking and he followed, and all along the street he was calling me a whore and a bitch in one breath and then the next he was telling me how much he loved me. But it made no difference. It was over. The closer we got to his road the more frantic he got, switching his words, switching his feelings, but it was just last minute hanging on, it did no good, it was over. I knew it, he knew it: over.

When we got to the top of his road he tried to drag me down there with him, pulling at me and pleading with his eyes at the same minute he's calling me a two-timing bitch getting off with Richard behind his back . . . There was a man came out the post office and stopped there, and watched us, and started to come over; Danny had no choice but to let me go.

'Well just fuck off then,' he shouted and he pushed me away, and stormed off down his road.

I step out of myself now to write this. I have to. I say this happened, and this. I piece it together, in the hope I might get a different picture somehow. Something more than just an end.

I walked on home, alone, thinking he'd come back. He'd be running up behind me, any second.

We couldn't just leave it like that, so *sudden*.

But he didn't come after me. By the time I got home the rain was running through my hair and onto my face, mixing up with the tears. There was a ripped-out numbness inside me, it started in my throat and worked down, deep below my heart.

I stuck my key in the front door in the vain hope that my mum might be out but as soon as she heard me she came flapping out from the living room calling, 'Who's that? Who's that?' like how many people could it be, letting themselves in with a key? In the background I could hear the jolly-jolly chit chat of daytime TV, of the sugared-up voices for the no-lifes, simpering on.

I dropped my stuff down on the floor and bent to take off my shoes, avoiding looking up at her.

'What are you doing home?' she barked, coming to a stop in the hall. Not too close. I spread my stuff out, my *wet* stuff, my jacket, my bag, the knackered remains of my umbrella, to keep her back.

'Boiler packed up,' I muttered.

'What boiler?'

'The *school* boiler.' I stayed down, ostensibly sorting out my stuff while she took this in. I didn't want her seeing my face, didn't want her asking questions. Out of the corner of my eye I could see her feet, standing there in her slippers, the blue veins bulging out on her ankle bones, the white, powdery skin.

'What time did this happen?'

'I don't know.'

'Well when did they send you home?'

'When we got there. There was a sign on the gates.' I wasn't thinking properly. Hadn't got my lies all lined up. But still, she'd have found out anyway, one way or another. A letter from the school, gossip from Mrs Crosby.

'What time is it?' she said, and to answer herself she dashed back to the door of the living room to see the TV; *Sally and Jo's Supermarket Savvy*, must be eleven-thirty. 'Then where have you been till now?' she demanded, padding back over to me.

'I went back to Cara's.' It was the best I could do. I'd wiped my face when she wasn't looking, got myself composed. I thought I'd look all right now but her hawk eyes homed right on in.

'What's the matter with you?' she demanded. 'Why are you so pale?'

'I'm *cold*.'

'Are you ill?' She stepped forward, stuck out a hand to put it on my forehead, like she did when I was little, to see if I was hot. I dodged her hand, and bent down again, to pick up my bag.

'It's the rain,' I said. 'That umbrella's had it.'

'Your eyes are red,' she accused. She was too close to

me now and I hated it. What is it when you spend half your life wanting someone to reach out to you and then when they do you back off, can't go there at all? She wanted to touch me but the only way she could do it was by treating me like a child, and I couldn't be touched by her any more. Just the thought of it had me recoiling. Out of nowhere I remembered some time when I was small, really small, about three or four and we were out somewhere, can't remember where; I'd got something on my face as kids do and she caught me by the arm, looked at me, and before I had time to realise what was happening she'd got out her hankie, spat on it and was rubbing at my cheek while I squirmed in horror. My God, the smell of that spit, coming at my face. How could that be cleaner than a little bit of chocolate or whatever? At three years old, an early memory: disgust.

'I've got a bit of a headache,' I said. 'That's all. Look, I'm going to go upstairs, get on with some coursework.'

I grabbed up my stuff and ran upstairs, leaving her standing there, confused. I didn't want to think about what she might be feeling, didn't want to think that she had any feelings at all. I couldn't deal with it.

In my room I sat on my bed and stared at myself in the mirror. Stared at my dark eyes, my white-out face.

How did it come to this?

All those words about forever, all those promises, those dreams . . . all nothing. All those things that I so, so wanted to believe, gone.

I'd put my phone down on the bed beside me. I wanted it to ring but at the same time I didn't. What could we say now? What was there left to say?

I'd taken to wearing the ring he gave me for my birthday on a chain around my neck; I took hold of it now, squeezed it so hard that the claws pressed dents into my fingers, but no great answers came, no revelation.

My whole life, everything, seemed like an empty, black hole.

That night I sat through dinner while my mum ranted on about the outrageousness of school boilers packing up and children being let loose to roam the streets when they should be stuck safely behind their desks. And in this weather, too.

'Don't they get it serviced?' she barked at me, like it was my fault. 'They ought to. They ought to keep it properly maintained so it *doesn't* break down.' She stuck a lump of chicken in her mouth and chewed it up, quick. 'Don't they, John?' she snapped at my dad, as soon as she'd swallowed. 'They ought to keep it maintained.'

'These things happen,' my dad replied, on the fence as ever.

'Kids sent off roaming the street. It isn't right.'

'I came home,' I said, prodding at the thing on my plate. It was some sort of pretend meat thing. Whatever it was I couldn't eat it. I couldn't eat anything.

'Not straight away, you didn't,' she said in her don't-you-argue-with-me, young-lady voice. 'Why aren't you eating your food?'

'I am.'

'No you're not, you're just poking at it.'

'I'm not hungry.'

'Why aren't you hungry? I had to hunt through the freezers in Quick-Mart to get you that. Soya, it is.'

'I've got a headache,' I said, staring at my plate. 'I told you.'

'A headache doesn't stop you eating.'

'I feel a bit sick.' I wished she'd just leave me alone. Or go back to moaning about the boiler. Anything other than sit staring at me like that.

But she was all suspicious now. 'What's this all about?' she demanded. 'Not that boy again, is it?'

I shook my head but I couldn't speak. I'd a mouthful of tears. Anyone with an *ounce* of sensitivity would have left it there, but not my mum.

'Are you pregnant?' she half shrieked suddenly,

dropping her knife and fork down with a clatter.

I stared at her now, and the tears spilled out. I couldn't *believe* her. 'No,' I bit out. 'I'm not pregnant.'

'Are you sure?'

'Of course I'm sure.'

'Don't think you're bringing a baby home here for me to look after if you've gone and got yourself in trouble!'

'For God's sake, is that all you care about?' I stood up, kicking my chair back behind me. It bashed against the sideboard, rattling the china, and she jumped up too, then.

'Mind what you're doing!' she yelled, flapping about a load of stupid old plates now.

'I'm not pregnant!' I screamed at her, to drum it home. I could hardly see for the tears pouring out my eyes, and the *anger*. 'I'm. Not. Pregnant. And if I was, do you think I'd tell you?'

I felt like I'd never stop crying.

I was lying on my bed, curled up on my side with my eyes shut so tight they felt stuck together. Downstairs my mum was screaming on at my dad, screaming, *Is this what I deserve? Is it? Sixteen years of my life I've given up for that girl and she just throws it back in my face. Wasting herself on that boy. If I find out she's lying to me . . .*

I pulled the pillow around my ears to try and muffle her out. I couldn't even hurt without her butting in, twisting it, making it worse. This is what I wanted to get away from, this is what I'd do *anything* to get away from.

My phone was still beside me, silent.

I'd pick it up and call Danny but what was the point? *He* hadn't called me. If I phoned him now I'd only end up hurting more and I couldn't stand it.

Him and my mum, they seemed the same right then, both of them, just hurting me all the time.

She sent my dad upstairs eventually.

He tapped on my door and I had to drag myself out of the oblivion that I'd cried myself into. I uncurled from my ball and lay flat, stretched out, away from him. The bed dipped by my feet as he sat down.

He sighed, and sighed again, as I did my best to pretend he wasn't there.

'Your mum's worried about you,' he said at last, and I could have laughed.

'She's got a funny way of showing it,' I muttered.

'Don't be like that now,' my dad said, standing up for her as always. 'She's got your best interests at heart. You know that.'

I didn't know anything of the kind, so I said nothing, and I just wished he'd go away.

No such luck. 'What's this all about then, pet?' he said. 'Not fretting over that boy, are you?'

'I'm not seeing him any more,' I said, just to get rid of him.

'Well, then,' my dad said brightly. 'I'm sure that's for the best.'

And he patted me on the leg, and trotted back off downstairs to tell the good news to my mum. Like that was that; sorted.

I must have fallen asleep and I woke up with a jolt; my phone had bleeped. He'd sent me a text. *Call me.* Then another: *I'm sorry.* And another: *I love you.*

I turned off my phone and lay back in the dark.

I didn't want to hear it any more.

14

I was late getting off for school the next day. I didn't want to go at all; I was hoping the boiler would still be broken but my mum, being my mum, had been on the phone first thing, finding out.

So if Danny had been waiting for me, he'd gone by the time I went by. And I hadn't put my phone on. We're not allowed them on in lessons anyway, so I didn't actually switch it on till lunchtime when I was hanging around in the loos because I'd got nowhere else to go. I didn't want to go out because I didn't want to risk seeing him. I couldn't cope, not yet.

And I just didn't want that feeling of having to look over my shoulder all the time, not knowing if he was there.

When I did switch my phone on, the messages came flashing up, one after another. *Call me. I love you. Please, don't push me away . . .*

He'd left one on my voicemail too; I was leaning back against the sinks trying to hear it when a load of Year Tens came crashing in. So I shut myself in one of the cubicles, as far away from them as possible, and crouched in there, phone pressed up hard against one ear, finger stuck in the other.

Just hearing his voice was a tug on my heart.

'*Forgive me, Louise,*' he said, and the tears started burning in my eyes, '*for every bad thing I've ever done. I never meant to hurt you, never. You're all I care about. In this whole fucked-up world you're the only thing that ever mattered to me. I'm nothing without you; please, don't turn away from me now . . .*'

I played it twice, three times, sitting on the edge of that loo seat with tears streaming down my face. I didn't even care if those girls out there could hear me crying. There was that note in Danny's voice, pulling at me all the time. I couldn't stand it. All this endless hurt going on and on. I just couldn't do it any more.

But that night I looked out my bedroom window just before I went to bed, and Danny was out there, sitting on that wall across the road looking up at me, like he'd been there for ages. As soon as I saw him my heart tripped over and started racing. He was *staring* up at my window; I could see his eyes, the glint from the street light.

Then he stood up, and crossed the road, and started walking up our drive. Panic started pumping out my heart now. It was just gone eleven; my mum had just gone to bed but my dad was still downstairs, pottering around in the kitchen. They'd do their nut if Danny called now, at this time. What was he thinking of?

I didn't know what to do. He was out of view now, too close to the house for me to see him. I just stood there, gripped, waiting for the doorbell to ring. It seemed like minutes went by. What was he doing? Was he waiting for me to sneak down and open the door to him? But how could I? Surely he could see the lights on downstairs? Surely he knew my parents were still up?

As quiet as I could I opened my bedroom door. My parents' room is right opposite mine; light shone out from under the door and I could hear my mum, still moving around. I crept across the landing to the top of the stairs, trying not to make the floorboards creak, and started tiptoeing down. All I could hope was that my dad didn't hear me and didn't come out from the kitchen, but what was I going to do if I did open the door? No way could I let Danny in.

I was almost at the bottom of the stairs and I could see his shadow through the glass of the front door. I could see him moving. Suddenly the letter box rattled and lifted and he stuck a letter through; it dropped onto the mat and I was there in a flash, picking it up. And then he left; I could hear him walking back up the path.

The kitchen door was part open and now it opened wider. 'That you, Louise?' my dad called, padding into the hall with his whiskey glass in his hand. 'I thought you were in bed.'

'I just wanted to check something,' I said, holding that letter behind my back. 'Something for school tomorrow.' And I was back up those stairs, fast as I could.

'What's going on?' my mum called out from across the landing but I ignored her; I was back in my room, door closed, straight for the window.

But he'd gone now. I strained my eyes, trying to get a glimpse of him out there in the dark, and I waited for ages in case he came back. But he didn't.

So I sat on my bed and opened the letter. It was a long letter, three pages; I've still got it, folded up small and hidden in my sock drawer with the rings he gave me and the little box with the dope inside. I can't bear to throw it away though I never read it any more. I don't need to; I remember it word for word.

His words lashed diagonally across the paper in a spider-thin scrawl. He'd listed everything we'd done together, written it like a story, a memoir . . . *Don't try and pretend it means nothing to you*, he wrote, *don't throw it all away. You know we're meant to be together for always, though the good times and the bad. I need you, Louise, we need each other. No one else will ever love you like I do, no one, not ever, no way . . .*

I was shaking as I read it. All these words, these desperate words, wrenching at my heart.

I'm going away. Don't ask me where to, I don't yet know and it doesn't matter. But there's nothing left for me here now. I can't live without you. If you care at all, if you ever want to see me again, meet me at the boathouse, tomorrow. One last time.

A tear dropped down onto the page, smudging his name. I turned it over and tried to blot it on my skirt but that just made it worse. My throat was so tight I couldn't swallow.

Of course I would meet him, I had to.

One more time.

I got out of maths the minute the bell went at the end of school and walked as fast as I could, all the way to the watersplash. It had stopped raining but turned even colder and my breath was coming hard and fast into the damp, foggy air. It had rained so much that the river was up and I panicked for a second; there was hardly any dry ground left down there off the bridge. Most of the reeds had died back and those that were left were swamped in water. I climbed down really carefully, keeping as close as I could to the bushes and trees, and trying not to sink into the mud. The further away from the bridge I got the worse it was; I squelched my way along, really scared now but you get to a point where you don't know whether to turn back or keep going. It was hard even to keep my balance and I pitched forward, clutching at whatever branches I could, more or less pulling myself along. Wet mud oozed inside my shoes, and my teeth were starting to clatter, with the cold, with fear, with this weird, driven feeling. I *had* to go on.

I had to say goodbye, properly. I owed him that. I owed it to us both.

So I pushed my way on, and in my head I had this running monologue: *You'll always be special to me, always. You're the first person I've ever loved. I'll never forget you, I'll never forget what we had together, and of course I'll always care . . .*

I got to the wire fence and my heart was knocking against my ribs, hard. Already it was getting dark. I tried to tell myself that was a good thing because I wouldn't be so visible, running across that lawn but my God the house looked spooky in the mist. Suddenly I remembered some really old film I saw once on TV, years ago, *The Hound of the Baskervilles* or something, about some terrifying dog, ripping people up in the fog. That film freaked me out so much it gave me nightmares. Why did I have to go and think of it now?

But I did think of it and panic bolted up my spine, stiffening me up. I was too scared to run, so I started tiptoeing, hoping the shadows from the trees would hide me but then I heard not so much a bark but a growl from that dog, close, and then another growl, getting closer. I quit trying to hide myself and ran for all my life across to the other side, through the trees and over the fence. And then I was thinking, *What am I doing, what if I don't even get there?* I was so, so wishing I hadn't done this now. And I was starting to chicken out; there was this little voice creeping into my head, saying, *Maybe it doesn't have to be goodbye after all, maybe we can sort it out . . .*

Danny was out of his head when I got there, sitting cross-legged on the boathouse floor, turning a knife over and over in his hands, that knife I'd got him in France. It was bitterly cold but he was sitting there just in his jeans and a T-shirt, and he'd cut his hand on the blade and got blood smeared across his hand and up his arm.

I'd been running so fast just a second ago but now I was stuck rigid, couldn't move, and the cold ripped down my throat as I breathed. He didn't look up. His head was tilted forwards, studying the knife as he played with it. He hadn't washed his hair for days. There were cigarette butts and joint roaches scattered all around him, and he'd been carving my name into the wooden floor, over and over, and he'd tried to write it in blood too, but the red had dried to brown and was already flaking away.

I didn't speak. I couldn't. I was locked to the spot, waiting. He knew I was there. Carefully, oh so carefully, he tossed the knife from one hand to the other, slowly at first and then faster, faster, from the left hand to the right and then back again till I was dazed from watching and then he flung it from his left hand and stuck out his right arm to meet the blade as it fell and cut into his skin. His hand clamped down on the knife and he pushed it in deeper. Blood oozed up and trickled over his arm and I snapped out of my trance.

'Stop it!' I screamed and I fell down beside him, down on my knees, with my hands on his arm. 'Please, stop it!' Blood made his skin sticky and I could feel it under my hands. He let the knife fall away and I looked into his face. He'd been crying at some point and the snot and tears had dried on his cheeks like rivers in the dirt. I looked in his eyes and bile was so thick in my throat I had to keep swallowing. I've been over it a thousand times in my head and I knew what was coming from the moment I looked into his eyes, knew it then and see it now, like a film in my head, playing again and again, stuck on repeat.

He flipped his arms round so he was clutching me. He knelt in front of me with his knees banged into mine and his hands hurting me through my sleeves; his breath was hot and sharp on my face. 'You . . . bitch . . . you . . . Judas . . .' he hissed at me. 'Why did you ignore my calls? Why do you just turn your back on me like that?' He spat the words into my face so I had to lean back, but he still had hold of my arms and wouldn't let go and we toppled over, sideways onto the slats. He slammed my arms out to my sides, pinning me down and looming over me. 'I trusted you. I gave everything to you. You can't just walk away from me.'

'I didn't just walk away,' I whispered. '*You* told *me* to fuck off.'

'But I called you. I sent you messages.' He dug his fingers into my arms and shook, hard. 'You fucking ignored me.'

'I didn't ignore you. I didn't know what to say.' My heart was punching out like a fist in my chest. 'What else *is* there to say?'

'Stay away from Richard,' he said. 'Do you hear me? Stay away from him or he's dead.'

'It's nothing to do with Richard.'

He was down on his elbows now; he raised one hand to run it through my hair and then he grabbed a handful and yanked. I screamed; he'd got both hands in my hair now, fingers scraping through the strands and pressing my skull.

'You're a liar,' he yelled into my face. 'You're a fucking liar.'

I couldn't move. He'd got my head tight in his hands. I thought I was going to die.

'You're like everyone else – you're a fucking liar.'

'I've never lied to you, Danny,' I managed to say, with the tears smarting out my eyes.

'It's you and me,' he spat. 'Don't you forget it. Don't you ever forget it. You and me.'

He pushed his face into mine in a sort of kiss, grinding his teeth into my lips and still squeezing my head so hard. His spit ran down my chin and I could hardly breathe. Then he loosened his grip and began to pat my head from side to side like a ball; the pats turned to hits and he lifted his face away. Immediately I started to howl; the hits became harder then I realised he was crying too, saying *You and me, Louise*, over and over. I put my hands up onto his chest and he stopped hitting me, and fell down into my arms, limp suddenly, half crushing me with his weight.

'Don't leave me,' he murmured into my neck. 'Please don't leave me.'

I held his head to my chest and cradled him there. His hair smelt of grease and cigarette smoke and the colour had all gone; it was matted and dull with dirt but I buried my face in it anyway. I stayed like that thinking the crying would stop; I held him so tight but it didn't end.

He put his hand on my breast, started touching me. 'You're all I've got,' he whispered. 'I can't live without you.'

He was kissing me now; my neck now, my face, and my eyes. My throat was so full of tears I couldn't speak, couldn't do anything except feel my heart speeding up again. The hand on my breast was working its way into my clothes; the other hand was still tangled in my hair but it was stroking my head now, and the back of my neck. It would be so easy to be lulled, to close my eyes and blank myself out. But not any more. Not now. We'd gone too far.

That knife was lying there on the slat beside us. I saw it, and I did a stupid thing. I moved too fast. I twisted under him and kicked the knife away before he could hold me still again; it fell with a plink into the water below. He lifted his head, sharp, stared at me. I pulled myself away before he could stop me, got halfway to my feet.

'I can't. Not any more. All this hurting all the time.' I was shouting, to convince him, to convince myself. 'It's no good, Danny. We're no good.'

I was almost standing. He started getting up; he reached out to grab me and I flung myself back. I must have stepped on a wonky slat or something because I lost my balance for a second. Adrenalin shot pins and needles down my arms and I twisted fast to save myself, but I'd forgotten how low the roof was and I caught the side of my head, *crack*, against a beam. Pain burst into my brain like an axe had gone in. I could feel myself falling, long after I hit the ground, falling like on a ferris wheel speeded up, like in a nightmare, going down and down. And I couldn't see. I'd got my eyes wide, wide open but I couldn't see anything except rush after rush of sparks, spinning out into the dark.

The film in my head stops, it starts again, it goes on and on. This is my hell; to forget, to never forget. Either way; this is my hell.

I could only have been out for seconds. I wanted to be out for ever, right out, but the pain started belting in, bringing me back and I was in this weird semi-place. He was kissing my face, such tiny, gentle kisses. I felt it like I was in heaven. And slowly, I could see him, a little blue at first, a little grey. I could see his face, so close to mine; the concern, the love in his eyes. I *was* in heaven. I was, for just a minute or two.

It hurt just to keep my eyes open. I didn't want to move my head; I felt like there was a giant staple in it, nailing it to the floor. He was leaning on his elbows, with the length of his body pressed up against mine. He was stroking my hair away from my face, away from the side of my forehead where I'd banged it, peeling away the hair where it was getting stuck. There was a tightness to my skin there; I could feel it when I blinked and when I frowned; sticky tight.

Danny's eyes connected with mine. 'I love you,' he said. 'Don't worry. I'll take care of you. You'll be all right.' And he started kissing my face again, and he kissed my head where it hurt. Kissed it so tenderly, like he didn't mind the blood.

There were tears running out of my eyes now and sliding sideways; on the hurt side I could feel them, cutting a path.

'Don't cry,' Danny said. 'We'll be all right now, you and me. We'll be all right.' I could feel his body trembling, like he was balanced on a nerve. 'You'll stay with me. I'll look after you.' He moved so he was on top of me, but carefully now, keeping his weight on his arms, and with him looking down at me like that I suddenly thought of that first time, up in my room with my parents downstairs, that first time we ever made love. And I didn't know what hurt most right then, my head or my heart but it seemed to me that we'd come full circle somehow. It seemed like the right way to end so this time when he kissed me I kissed him back. I was wearing my black jacket over my school stuff, open; he pushed it aside and started kissing my neck, moving down inside the front of my shirt. His hands were on my body, all over, touching me like he was blind, pressing the memory into his skin.

I don't know what I was thinking, what I was doing. Just that it was an end. My head was screaming with goodbye.

'I love you,' he was saying, over and over, 'God I love you.' And I could feel that love as he struggled with my clothes, feel it in the heat of his skin against mine. I *wanted* to feel it, one last time. What difference would it make now?

But it was the coldest, coldest thing. It was all his love, not mine. And what kind of love? He collapsed on top of me and I knew it was a mistake. To me it was goodbye, but he'd never see it like that, never.

'Stay with me,' he said afterwards, while I lay underneath him on the slimy, rotten wood, with the damp stiffening into my bones. I was shivering from the cold now, and from this weird sickness that felt like it was something to do with the throbbing in my head. He was on top of me still, with his arms around me, holding me, his weight pinning me down. I could see in his eyes that nothing had changed, but then I knew that it never would. He'd never let me go, never. He'd have me with him forever, slamming into the dark.

There was a nail digging into my back and I tried to move a little; Danny's arms locked tighter around me. It was pitch dark now, and late, though I didn't know how late, and I didn't dare look at my watch. My mum would be throwing a fit. I hadn't even told her I was going to be late, and I'd switched off my phone.

'Stay,' he said again, sharper.

'I – I'm cold,' I said. 'And my head hurts.'

He stared down at me, not moving.

'And something's sticking in my back.'

'I won't let you go,' he said.

'I know.'

Slowly, he eased himself off. But he kept his eyes locked with mine, and one arm across my chest, and one leg still laid across mine. I held his gaze as I tried to get my clothes back together. And then I lay still, very still.

'You'll stay here with me.'

My heart was thumping out a hole inside my chest. His eyes were black, blacker still in the dark now.

'We can't stay here, Danny,' I said. 'We've nothing to eat. We'll freeze.'

He said nothing, just stared at me, and that leg over mine got heavier.

I felt the tears flooding back into my eyes. 'Look at us, Danny,' I said. 'We *can't* stay here. *You* can't stay here.'

'Then we'll run away,' he said. 'Now. You and me. We'll get away from all this shit.'

His eyes were wide, unblinking. I swallowed, and swallowed again.

'It won't work, Danny.' Still he stared at me. I wanted to look away but I couldn't. I could see myself in the black of his eyes, my frightened face, distorted.

'Yes it will. We'll be all right away from here. We'll be all right on our own.'

'We've got nowhere to go.'

The arm he'd got across my chest stiffened and he grabbed my arm with his hand, and shook, hard. I felt it right into my head. 'Just stop your fucking excuses,' he shouted, right in my ear. 'I'm out of this place. Fucking out of it and you're coming with me.'

I felt like I was going to be sick. I turned my head away from his, tried to breathe, slow. My head was throbbing, throbbing.

'You're all I've got,' he was saying. 'I'll never let you go, never. I'll fucking die first. I will, I'll kill myself if you try and leave me.' And he kept on saying these things, over and over. He'd die. We'd both die. We'd both be better off dead.

I was staring out the boathouse door. It was so dark out there. I could hear the wind hissing through the trees, and other sounds; I don't know what.

'We'll need money,' I said and my voice came out thin, empty. His fingers were digging into my arm. I turned my head back to face him. 'We'll need money and . . . things.'

'We don't need anything,' he said.

'We do, Danny. Look . . . You're right. So many bad things have happened lately. We've just got to get away.'

He was watching me, eyes narrowed.

'But if we haven't got any money we'll end up coming straight back.'

'I'm never coming back,' he said.

'We need money, then. I could go home, get some. And I could get my passport. And some clothes. I can't go far in my school stuff. And listen, my mum always leaves her purse in the kitchen; she'll have some money and I could nick her credit card. We can go anywhere, then.' I was talking too fast, thinking he'd never believe me, but I carried on, spouting out all these plans because I couldn't think what else to do. And eventually he sat up and started digging around in his pocket for his fags but the packet was squashed now and when he tipped it up there was only one left. He pulled it out and tried to straighten it.

'You got any?' he said.

I shook my head. 'I could get some. On my way back. I'll stop at the off licence.'

He twisted that cigarette between his fingers. I could see him, thinking, working it out. Slowly I sat up, and tried to ignore the weird, sliding feeling inside my head.

'If I let you go you won't come back.'

'I will, Danny. Trust me. Please. I'll be back in half an hour, less.'

I was kneeling now, ready to run. He was staring at me hard, fingers toying with that cigarette. Light it, I was thinking, go on, just light it.

'Promise you'll come straight back,' he said.

'I promise,' I said, and I leant forward, and kissed him.

'You won't let me down.'

The blood was roaring in my head. 'I won't let you down.'

I ran like there were witches at my heels. I had to get as far away as I could, before he changed his mind. My head felt like it was splitting open but I daren't slow down for even a second. I was terrified he was going to come running up behind me. Intuition had me finding the right way back, too driven by my own fear to be scared of the dark. I ripped my fingers and my knees on the barbed wire, getting through the fence, but I didn't feel it. All the pain I had was in my head and in my heart, thumping out.

By the time I got back to the road I was drenched in mud from all the times I'd slipped and fallen, but I still didn't stop. I still thought he'd be behind me, any second. I could hardly see for crying out of control and every breath cut raw into my chest. God knows how I made it home, but I did, and the first thing I saw was the police car, parked outside our house. Relief and panic hit me at the same time. I staggered on jelly legs up the path; I slammed my hand down on the door bell, heard it ring and ring.

My dad opened the door. I saw his face change from white-out worry to something way, way worse. And then I felt his arms around me, folding me in.

I was standing in the hall, like no one knew what to do with me. There was my dad, my mum and the policeman, all staring at me, all talking, except for my mum who had started screaming the moment she saw me. I could see their mouths moving, but all I could hear was this clamour; that scream pitching on, and this other roaring sound starting up inside my head and there was this rushing feeling coming up from the floor, tipping me backwards. I wanted just to close my eyes. Someone grabbed a chair from the kitchen and sat me down on it. Then they were all bent down, staring at me, staring at my head.

'That's a nasty bash you've had there,' the policeman said and his face loomed in and out, blurring at the edges. He'd already got his notepad out, and he was asking me all these questions. His voice came at me slow, too slow, like I was speeded up and slowed right down again all at the same time. Could I tell him where I'd been? Could I tell him what had happened? And behind him my mum was repeating him in this high-pitched, screeching echo: *Where've you been? What's happened to you? Where've you been? Oh my God, oh my God what's happened?*

And on and on.

And there was my dad with his face saying, 'What happened to you, pet?' and I felt like I'd slammed into a wall. You never think this will happen. You never think you'll go *too far*.

'What happened to your head?' the policeman was asking me again and again in this slow careful voice, like he thought I couldn't understand. I had to tell them; I had no choice.

'I banged it,' I said and my tongue was thick like dead meat in my mouth.

'What did you bang it on?' he asked.

'The roof.'

'What roof?'

'The boathouse roof.' *The boathouse roof.* I don't know how I said it. That special, secret place. Out now. *Over.*

'Must have been a low roof,' he said. They were all silent now, staring at me, my mum and my dad. I tried not to look at them. 'So where is this boathouse?'

'Down the river. By the watersplash,' I whispered and I thought of him there, waiting for me.

'And what were you doing at the boathouse?'

I stared at him, at his brown eyes.

'I was with my boyfriend.'

My mum jumped like she'd been stung. 'That boy? You were with that boy?' Her hands were on her face, they were in her hair, they were on her face again, her bright red face, bug-eyed, screaming at me. 'He's done this to her!' she shrieked. 'Oh my God he's done this!'

'Quiet, Gillian. Quiet. We don't know,' my dad said, or something like that. I couldn't actually hear him because they were all talking at once again.

'It was an accident,' I said but I didn't know if it made any difference. I didn't even know if they heard me.

The policeman was in fast-forward now, winding up. 'What's your boyfriend's name?' he asked.

'Danny,' I said. It was out of my control now; I could feel myself, sliding.

'Danny who?'

'Danny Fisher.'

'And where does Danny live?'

He was writing it all down. I could feel myself sinking deeper and deeper. This could not all be real.

'Three Acacia Avenue,' I said. 'It wasn't his fault. I stood up too quick and banged my head. It was an accident.'

'Right then,' the policeman said, standing up to go.

'What are you going to do to him?' I asked quickly.

'Nothing I can do if you say it was an accident.' He put his notepad away, and his hand on the front door to open it. 'Think I'll go and find this Danny Fisher, though. See what he has to say.' He nodded to my parents, who were both standing there looking like they'd been slapped. 'Better get that cut seen to,' he said.

The minute the policeman had gone they shuffled me off of that chair and into the kitchen and plonked me down at the table. Under the light.

'I knew this would happen!' my mum was screaming, snatching up random spoons and cups and anything else left lying around the kitchen, and dumping them back down with a crash somewhere else. 'I knew it! How am I to know where she is when she lies to me all the time? I knew it would end like this, I knew it!'

My dad was looking at my head, close up. I could feel his fingers tentatively moving my hair. 'This is deep,' he said. 'It needs cleaning.'

'I've been going out of my mind because of you, young lady,' my mum wailed, like my head didn't hurt enough already. 'I had to call the police because of you! Do you know how long you'd been missing? Do you? Four hours and eighteen minutes! Four hours and eighteen minutes since you should have been home from school! Four hours and eighteen minutes that I have been going out of my mind!'

'Get some water,' my dad snapped. 'And something to clean this with.'

But she didn't, so he had to get it himself. He got a tea towel, out the drawer.

'Not that!' my mum shrieked. 'Don't get blood on that!'

He ran the tea towel under the tap, and dabbed at my head so gently with his shaking hand that it made me cry even more. 'Hush, pet,' he said. 'Hush.' Like I was five years old again, and fallen off my bike. There was no colour in his face at all; I'd done that.

'Did Danny do this to you, pet?' he asked.

'No,' I said and the tears were chugging down my

face. 'I banged it on the roof. He loves me, Dad; he didn't want to let me go.'

'All right, pet. All right,' he said and my mum snapped, 'All right! It's not bloody all right,' and slammed a pan down onto the counter but missed, and it fell off and clattered on the floor, metal against stone.

I felt like I'd never stop hurting, never for the rest of my life.

'I think we better get you to the hospital,' my dad said.

15

I needed a few stitches, that's all.

I thought I'd be out of there once it was done but they made me wait for ages, and that was on top of the original wait to be seen. Two different nurses came in to look at me, and a doctor. And they all had the same questions. It was like they thought if a different person asked me, they might get a different answer.

I told them the truth, though not all of it. I had to. The truth wasn't as bad as the things their imaginations were thinking up.

'How did this happen?' the first nurse asked, cutting the hair away from my cut so she could get at it better.

'I banged it on a roof.'

'Got some splinters in here.'

'It was a wooden roof.'

The second nurse came in. I saw them exchange looks. 'Ouch,' she said to me when she saw my cut. 'How did you get that?'

'I *banged* it.' How many times was I going to have to say it? I saw them glance at each other again, over their tray of tricks. I just wanted to get stitched up and out of there. All I could think of was Danny, sat out at the boathouse, waiting for me.

He'd know by now, surely. He'd know I was never coming back.

'Must have been something hard,' one of them muttered.

'It was. It was a roof.'

'Here we go then,' the first nurse said, threading up her needle. 'Dad waiting outside, is he?' she asked, and like it was a cue the other one went out the cubicle to check on him. 'Don't worry,' the one left behind with the needle said. 'You'll hardly feel a thing.'

She was lying, but what did I care?

I could smell her peppermint breath as she stuck her needle in and out, and she was humming under her breath. 'Were you on your own when it happened?' she asked, like it had just occurred to her.

'No,' I said. 'I was with my boyfriend. My ex-boyfriend.'

That needle went in and out, fast, neat; I could hear the weird sound of the cotton pulling tight. 'Did you have a bit of a fight, then?'

'No.'

That needle stopped in midair. 'Want to tell me what happened?'

'I slipped. I fell. I banged my head.'

'Was it very muddy there, then, where this roof was? And did you hurt your hands at the same time?'

They switched over, and I got the other nurse back, cleaning up the scratches on my hands and my knees.

'What happened here?' she asked, wiping ointment on my knees.

I tried not to wince. 'I caught them on a fence.'

She raised her eyebrows.

'There was barbed wire. I didn't see it,' I said.

'Must have been in a hurry,' she said, and then, 'Was this before or after you banged your head?'

'After.'

'Boyfriend with you, was he?'

'When?'

'When you caught your knees on the fence.'

'No. He – he stayed behind.'

She nodded, like she understood. Then when she'd finished patching me up she said, 'Is there anything else I need to know about?' looking me square in the eyes. 'Did anything else happen to you when you fell?'

I know what she meant. In my hurry, I'd done up my shirt wrong, and they'd all noticed. And besides, doctors and nurses can probably smell sex a mile off; they're trained that way.

'No,' I said, and she sighed.

'You're making a mistake if you think you should protect him, this boyfriend,' she said.

I could hear my dad, almost shouting, out there in the corridor. My dad, who never raised his voice.

'She's just turned sixteen. She's a *child*.'

And I could hear another voice, hushed; I couldn't hear the words.

'Well when will he be here?' my dad demanded. I could hear his frustration and I closed my eyes.

I felt guilty as hell. I felt like it would never end.

Then the doctor came in, and sat on the edge of the bed.

'That was a nasty gash you got there,' she said, looking at my stitches. 'You better take it easy for a day or two.'

I could see my dad's feet, under the curtain. I wondered why he had to wait out there, and then I realised; they probably thought I'd find it easier to talk, with him out the way. I just wanted to go home. I just wanted to crawl into my bed and bury myself in the dark.

'What's your boyfriend's name?' she asked.

'Danny.'

'Did he do this to you?' she asked, quietly, gently. She put her hand on my leg, a motherly pat. I could feel the tears brimming up in my eyes.

'No,' I said, because he hadn't. I'd done it all to myself.

'Then why the tears?' she asked.

'I want to know where he is. He said he'd run away. He said he'd *kill* himself.'

'People sometimes say these things but it doesn't mean they're going to do them,' she said, but what did she know? She didn't know a thing about Danny.

It seemed like I'd been there for hours. I was so, so tired now. I could hear my dad again, talking to someone, doing his best to keep his voice down. I watched his feet, agitatedly pacing about, moving in and out of view beneath that curtain. Every now and again he came in and said something like *All right, pet, we'll be off soon* but he didn't hang around. He'd be back out in that corridor again, pacing.

Danny would have given up waiting for me ages ago. I wondered if they'd found him and I hoped that they had because I was scared what he'd do if they didn't. I didn't want him running away with no money and no clothes to God knows where, or worse; I couldn't even think about worse. But if they did find him would he understand that I had to tell them where he was, for both our sakes? Would he understand that I had no choice?

Someone started to open the curtain and I was

thinking it would be one of those nurses yet again, but it wasn't. It was that policeman come back to tell me they'd found him.

Danny hadn't come after me. He hadn't run away or killed himself. He'd still been sat there, waiting for me.

It broke my heart to think of it. It broke my heart to think of him looking up and seeing them, instead of me.

I kind of thought that would be it.

But everything I'd said before I had to say again. That I'd slipped and banged my head, that it was an accident. That I hadn't been hurt or pushed or forced into anything. Often I wonder what would have happened if I had let them blame Danny. They all wanted to blame him; the policeman, my mum, my dad. They wanted assault pinned on him; they wanted rape. I know that.

Stuck in that hospital at gone two in the morning, tired and so strung out, it would have been a whole lot easier to just say yes to all those leading questions and let him get all the blame.

But I'd gone to the boathouse because I'd wanted to. I'd made love to him one last time because I'd wanted to. The banged head and the scraped knees – what did they matter compared to everything else?

It was goodbye and he didn't want to hear it. How could I ever blame him for that?

I asked the policeman what they were going to do with him but he dodged the question.

'That young man's caused an awful lot of bother,' he said. 'Not least of all to his mother. We want to be sure it's not going to happen again.'

Just before he left he said, 'Did you know he'd been smoking cannabis?'

I just looked at him. Of course I knew. He *knew* I knew.

'You've had a lucky escape, young lady,' he said.

16

My mum said the same thing, every chance she got.

'You've had a lucky escape, my girl,' said in exactly the right tone to imply that it wasn't an escape but an outrage. That I'd got off scott free, and that I should be suffering somehow, more than I already was.

They'd let Danny off with a caution, and put him on a list for psychiatric help. And he was to stay away from me. I know that, because my mum rammed it down my throat, every chance she got.

'Don't you go thinking he'll be coming round here again,' she gloated, when she caught me looking out the front room window. 'The police have put paid to that, good and proper. If that boy so much as looks at you he's in trouble. Do you hear me? And I mean *trouble*.'

I was off school for a couple of days with my sore head but there was no chance of any rest, not with my mother on at me the whole time.

'I knew he wasn't right in the head,' she said and I tried not to flinch. 'He ought to be locked up!'

I turned away from the window, but she was blocking

the door. Did she have any idea how I felt? I mean, really, did she have a *clue*?

'He'd been taking drugs!' she burst out, and this, of course, was the biggest crime. 'Yes that's right! Drugs! Did you know that? Did you?' And then, like the possibility had only just dawned on her, 'If I ever find out that *you've* been taking drugs, my girl, I'll . . .'

I couldn't get past her that way so I turned to get out the other door instead, into the kitchen.

'You've brought this all on yourself,' she yelled after me, as if I didn't know it. 'Let that be a lesson to you.'

Later, I stood in my room, and looked out of the window there, where she couldn't see me. Stupidly, I still half expected Danny to come wandering up the street and sit himself on that wall under the tree opposite, like he had so many times. I couldn't quite get my head round the fact that he wouldn't, not ever again.

When you love someone you think it'll go on forever, in the beginning. Then when it starts to end you think the ending will go on forever. You never think that it'll ever be *nothing*, totally stopped, gone. It was like there was this great gap where my heart had been, and it hurt. And I looked out that window and I tried to focus on that tree, but all I could see was my reflection in the glass and all I could feel was this great flatness, coming out of my head and stretching before me forever and ever.

But even up in my room I got no peace. No peace to *grieve*. They wouldn't let me out of their sight for more than a second, my mum and my dad, and I couldn't stand it. I wanted to be on my own. I wanted to just hide away and hurt in private but they'd be banging on my door, opening it uninvited, checking on me. Especially my mum.

'No good feeling sorry for yourself now,' she said. 'You've no one to blame but yourself.'

And I just looked at her and thought well hang on a minute, how come it's all my fault now? Looking at her, with her mouth all tight and a nerve flickering away under her left eye, you'd think she'd had all her nightmares about me come true. I'd proved myself to be what she always thought I was; no good.

It was all round the school that Danny Fisher had gone psycho.

I walked back in and there it was for all to see: the evidence. The stitches looked awful, tight, purple and red, like something out of a horror film. I'd have kept a plaster stuck over them only it kept catching and pulling on the stubble where the hair was growing back, after they'd cut it away. So I had to go around with everyone gawping at me, and speculating, like they thought I couldn't hear.

'Did you see her head?'

'Danny Fisher did that. Flipped his lid. Smacked her one.'

'I heard it was a hammer.'

'I always knew he was a fucking nutter.'

I tried not to hear. I told myself I just had to get through it.

I felt like I was under a spotlight, naked.

I had to go to the headmaster's office, straight after registration. Mrs Neil told me, right in front of everyone, like they weren't all staring at me enough already.

'Mr Parry would like to see you, Louise,' she said. 'At nine-fifteen.'

I stared at my desk, while everyone else stared at me. This would be the same Mr Parry, who had never so much as acknowledged me before, in my whole six years at the school, and now he couldn't wait to see me. Still, I'd known it was coming. My parents had been in to see him while I was off school. Probably Danny's mum had been in too. And the police, for all I knew. And whoever else was involved. All putting their bit in.

The upshot was Danny wouldn't be coming back, not for a long while at least. My mum had taken great pleasure in telling me that. 'Don't you think you'll be seeing that boy at school,' she'd ranted at me, pointing her finger in my face. 'Oh no, he won't be going back there again, not for a long time. Never, if I have anything to do with it!'

'Ah, Louise,' Mr Parry said, checking my name on his notes when I walked in. 'You're doing your GCSEs this year. Very important time.'

I sat down. It was obvious to me that he didn't know what to say. But then why would he? He didn't even know who I was, until now.

'It's very important that you work hard. Knuckle down. Do your best.' He tapped his pen on the piece of paper in front of him, looking at me over his glasses. And he sighed. I think the sigh was supposed to make me think he cared. 'Put recent events behind you,' he said at last, in this vaguely fatherly tone. 'Move on.' He sat back in his chair, looking at me. 'You've your future to think about.'

I stared at his desk, and said nothing.

'It's not our school policy to exclude pupils unless absolutely necessary.' He was drumming that pen again. 'But it *is* our policy to take a very hard line on drugs. In view of this I must tell you that . . .' he checked his notes again '. . . Daniel Fisher will not be returning to this school in the foreseeable future.'

He paused, and I sat there rigid, brittle as glass. Was that all that mattered to him? Did he think that was all this was about? A bit of dope? And did he think Danny would even care? He was hardly ever at school anyway. I mean, how can you kick out someone who's never there? Someone who lives on a different planet entirely? I could feel tears stinging at the backs of my eyes and I focused on the phone on his desk, staring so hard that it hurt, to keep them back. I didn't *want* to sit there crying like a naughty little girl in the headmaster's office.

He was waffling on. 'In view of your promising academic achievement, blah, blah, blah . . .'

Truth is, if he kicked out everyone who'd done drugs he'd end up with no one left. But what was the loss in kicking out Danny? He was never there anyway; what great loss would he be to the league tables?

And meanwhile Danny is wherever he is, far away from me.

Mr Parry was banging on about all of us at Eppingham High working together for the common goal, or some such bullshit; I tried to switch off my ears. But then he said these words that stuck themselves on me whether I wanted them to or not: 'You've been given a second chance, Louise. Don't waste it.'

* * *

I'd no choice but to go trailing around with Cara and Emma again, and you can imagine how awful that was. I swear they only put up with me out of pity, and the worse thing was I was grateful for that pity. No one else wanted to go near me.

Cara was still going out with Jacob. It turned something over inside of me to see them all loved up, so solid with each other. Of course she only put up with me if she wasn't with him, which meant no weekends, no out of school hardly at all to speak of. And if I was with her at school, at lunchtime say, and he came over, I'd have to go. She never said so as such, but it was understood. *I* understood. Some things just can't be forgiven. And then I'd have to watch them from a distance, so easy with each other, so straight forward, so unlike me and Danny.

And boy, you should have seen Emma gloat, now that she and I had had our roles reversed. She must have been loving all this, and one way or another I got my face rubbed in it every day. Plans made that didn't include me. Chats about things they'd done at the weekend that didn't include me. Last minute lunchtimes with Jacob and Miles, that didn't include me.

I didn't complain. How could I? I was a charity case; I had to take what I was given.

* * *

It was the weirdest Christmas. I hardly went anywhere and I didn't see anyone. My mum didn't want the family seeing the state I'd gone and got myself into.

'You can't see people looking like that!' she shrieked. 'What on earth do you suppose they'll think?'

'They'll think I banged my head,' I said, though I couldn't care less if we saw my aunt and uncle and cousins or not. On the rare occasions we did see them there was always some little drama. My mum would find something to get in a hump about. Something somebody said, something somebody didn't say. There was always something. And I could never forget the incident with the plates. As far as I was concerned it was my mum that was the embarrassment, not me.

So it was a quiet Christmas, with just us and my gran, and my mum's omnipresent bad mood.

And when school started again I had to hear all about the wonderful time had by Cara and Emma, and Cara and Jacob, and I had to admire the silver bracelet that Jacob had given Cara and that she wore all the time now, and fiddled with in lessons, gazing dreamily into space.

It did my head in.

The thing is with Danny I'd felt so alive, so balanced on a knife edge all the time, and now I felt halfway to dead. The stuff before Danny and the stuff to come after was just a grey mass of nothingness. I looked back to before I met him and I just saw the endless day in, day out dreary boredom. I'd rather die than go back to that. But what would I do now, without him? Finish school, go to college, get a job, a husband, a kid and wind up like my own mother?

Again, I'd rather die. Believe me, I'd rather die.

Every morning when I walked past his road on my way to school my heart would start hammering up. I thought he'd be there, one day. Not going to school but, you know . . . I wanted to just run into him somehow and then I could say *hi, how are you?* and he might say the same thing back. And I'd see that he was fine again now. Perfectly OK. And maybe we could even be friends.

But it never happened. And I was only fooling myself anyway. How could we ever be friends?

A couple of times I walked up his road, though I don't know why I had to go on torturing myself. It was like picking at a scab that needed to heal. But I'd sneak along, dodging behind trees and cars, with the blood pounding in my head, terrified I'd see him, terrified I wouldn't.

And sometimes I'd press YAMIE on my phone and watch his number come up but I always hung up before it rang. I should have just deleted his number. I should have, but I didn't.

Weeks, months later I still kept expecting him to turn up outside my window at night. I still expected him to not give up. He'd want an explanation; why did I leave him that night and not come back? Why did I send the police instead?

And I wanted to explain. That's what ate me up more than anything. I wanted to put the full stop at the end of the line, have it closed, but it wouldn't be, not ever. One full stop would need to be followed by another and then another. I'd never get to explain; he'd never get to hear. And it had to be like that.

It was over. Finally, totally over. I told myself this.

Slowly, it sank in.

Once I ran straight into Richard, on the way out of school. It was kind of awkward bumping into him like that; I hadn't spoken to him, not since that last time, with Danny. I didn't know what to say to him now other than had he seen Danny lately? Did he know how he was?

'Don't really see him,' Richard said, with a shrug. 'He goes round with Bez most of the time.' And that was it. He stood there, I stood there. Then he shrugged again. 'See you, then,' he said, and walked away.

I didn't try to speak to Richard again, after that. If I walked past him I pretended I hadn't seen him. We'd nothing in common before Danny, and we'd nothing in common now, after. He was from a different time, a different world. And I could feel that world curling in on itself, and dying.

I'd had one interview at Meadlands but after my GCSE results came out I had to have another, because my grades weren't good enough.

My mum had had a field day. 'You silly girl!' she'd yelled at me. 'Throwing yourself away on that boy! Wasting yourself! You don't deserve to do well.'

I really believe she was glad I'd done so bad. I'd got my comeuppance, as she'd say.

It was the same guy who'd interviewed me the first time. He had a file on the desk in front of him and he took a letter out of it, and read it while I sat there. I could see my school's name on the letterhead, and I could just imagine what was written there. *Goes around with the wrong sort of boys*, that kind of thing.

He looked at me hard while he flicked that letter with his thumb.

'Your art teacher speaks very highly of you,' he said, and then he paused, and sat there looking at me for what seemed like a very long time. 'You'd have to work very, very hard,' he said at last. And he paused again. My heart was in my mouth. 'And I suggest you re-sit your maths and your English next year.'

He gave me a place. That's all that mattered. I didn't care if I had to re-sit all my GCSEs. From Meadlands I could go on to art school, get a diploma or something . . . I was out of here, so, so out of here.

And when I started in September there were only a handful of people from my school there, and not a single one of them was in any of my classes.

Some of the people doing art were older; they'd already been to college or done other things before. It was totally unlike school. You could come and go as you needed. There was no nine o'clock check-in, no one to keep you locked up till four. So long as you went to your classes no one cared. On Tuesdays I only had one class all day, in the afternoon, but usually I'd go in early and go straight to the art studio, and just paint for hours. You could do that. You could leave your work out. You could come and go.

And the best thing was that no one knew me. No one knew about Danny. I didn't have it written on a placard above my head any more: *Nutter's property. Keep off!*

I could put it behind me. I could reinvent myself.

* * *

And then I saw him again.

It was in Swanley. I was going into college late one day and I thought I'd go for a wander around the shops before I caught the train. I'd just walked into the shopping precinct and I saw him straight away, coming towards me; he was wearing his jeans and a white shirt and he looked like he always did. And he was with a girl, walking with his arm around her. He was smiling.

My heart started racing like there was an express train inside my chest. I ducked into a shop doorway, with every nerve in my body jangling. It was so weird seeing him with another girl, but what had I expected? That he'd be pining for me still? And surely it was good that he was smiling. Maybe he was different with her, maybe he was OK.

I was glad that he'd moved on. Of course I was.

Even so, I stayed hidden in that shop till they'd long gone past, and then I went straight off the other way to catch the next train to college.

I didn't look back.